A Life Reborn and Renewed

The Story of Alex Gross in His Own Words,
Thoughts, Ideas and Lessons

Edited and Compiled by
Ty G. Busch Ph.D.
With the Assistance of
Justin Peeples

Foundation for International Rights and a New Day

Trafford rev. 04/25/2011

 www.trafford.com

North America & international
toll-free: 1 888 232 4444 (USA & Canada)
phone: 250 383 6864 ♦ fax: 812 355 4082

Table of Contents

Dedication

I met Alex Gross while living in Georgia and teaching at Kennesaw State University, and felt immediately motivated to honor his life and struggle, and to make his story known to as many people as possible. I had asked him to speak at several classes over the years that I knew him, and as one of my mentors, he helped me to come out in proclaiming Judaism as the faith of my father and extending another branch of the Tree of Life to my family.

Alex Gross and my father were both self-made men. Alex had the advantage of European education outside theology. My father's education was theological after he was granted sanctuary by the Jesuits, though he did not have the advantage of long history of formal schooling. His Judaism was erased by falsified baptismal documents to elude the Nazis. Alex lost track of his family during the holocaust and was fortunate that his brothers helped him come to come to America and regain what he lost as a result of his experience in the holocaust. His marriage to his first wife made him strong in his commitment to his role as a family man and his restarted family, only to end tragically when her life would be taken from him by a murderer. However, I find his ability to overcome such great trauma, which erased much of his childhood, to be the lasting mark of this stoically humble man.

I had learned of my father's hidden past about the time my father was dying. This gave me strength to know how powerful my own past was. A past my brother disregarded, interpreting my interest as another attempt of me trying to make over my life. I took my brother's comments as a measure of how our relationship deteriorated. I decided to honor my father's past by giving survivors of the Holocaust, of Vietnam, of Darfur, and of Apartheid a bond with many who have never had to endure such tragic hardships. Out of these group encounters were many that had fathers in Vietnam, parents in Darfur or South Africa. As human beings we have all had experiences which make us as a group a unique part of human kind.

For myself, Alex's story is like a lesson out of Tuesdays with Morrie. I was the student coming to the professor I had learned to love. I approached Alex as I did once my father who gave me good, reasonable directions & life lessons. I had never got to do that with my father before he died. Alex was there for me when my relationship with the Mormons deteriorated, and a church leader partnered with an evil man who was bent on destroying me. He was there for me as I later evolved into a messianic Jew, embracing openly the traditions of my father's past even before my excommunication from the Mormon church was final. Although Alex was not terminally ill like the character Morrie, he was nevertheless a man with great energy, living every day as if it were his last.

What his writings represent of Alex Gross the man, time and circumstance will only tell. The Holocaust survivors have been declining in numbers and so to have been declining in importance. I feel it's important that we remember them as persons, and to remember and commemorate them annually. One of the most important things we can do is remember the events that preceded the terrible tragedies, whether they are the Holocaust, Apartheid, Iraq, Darfur, or anywhere. We can draw on the Significance of this work if we are willing to do more, because each offers a new pane of glass in the mosaic of the frail human condition which breeds hate and indifference.

There are many men I have known in life, but none ever turned over to me their life story after many writings and rewritings and said to publish it without making a big profit. His story was the most personal part of mine & my wife's experience with Alex. He once said to us that this was his therapy, however I saw it as a man trying to reconnect his life. I now know that trauma during a person's life disjoints the inner child in all of us. We react to trauma by trying to blame ourselves. Alex did this to a certain extent, as we could all expect, asking himself such questions as "what could I have done different that might have avoided all of what I just experienced?" I am not going to take issue with his words. I am going to expand what I saw, and emphasize on those things that I want survivors, the general public and countless generations to read and ponder. He invited me to be a part of his writer's colloquium, and during my time there I saw a man relentless to remember every word, event and error he might have made during this time. My contribution will be the period of time I knew him and what I feel he is trying to get you to see from his thoughts, words and ideas.

I now invite you to read his account.

Special Acknowledgement

I am indebted to Justin Peeples, a person I blessed with the task of co-editing this work, and assisting me in formulating and clarifying the Dedication and Foreword which serve to set this work apart, due to the particular ground that was covered. Justin was hired through an economic stimulus grant, and worked under my supervision on this project.

Introduction
by
Justin Peeples & Ty G. Busch PhD

I consider it a personal tragedy that I never had the pleasure of speaking with Alex Gross personally. In addition to the difficulties this presented in compiling his story, I also feel a degree of disappointment that I never got to know the man who had lived through these extraordinary times, and worse still, to hear how much more he surely had to say. More than in the events and facts he recalls, the way he moved from one topic to another speaks volumes of what he remembers most fondly, terribly, and vividly in a way that a simple recorded history never can.

The account of any survivor of Hitler's atrocities is, of course, exceptional in any right, not simply for the extent of the events as they happened, but for the sake of each individual's personal perspective on it as well. Who they were, who they became, what they lost, what they came to gain through their hardships, all of these stories are told in their personal narratives of how they endured under Hitler's regime. The history of the war is fascinating in its own right, of course, but what stays with you is the personal stories, filled as they inevitably are with the private touches, both stated and suggested, that remind you of the central humanity within them. It's not sufficient to remember tragedies as merely a sequence of historical events; the what, where and when. Rather, we must remember them as a collection of lives affected; the who, how and why.

As I said, not having Mr. Gross to consult with presented challenges in assembling his story, but I hope that you will be able to take away from reading it at least as much as we have in reading and writing it, absorbing his unique perspective, his individual past, and the myriad other details, large and small, that make this story uniquely his own.

Chapter 1: Childhood Memories

I was born on September 18, 1928, the sixth son to our mother and father in the same ordinary fashion as any other kid in our area. I was reared in an orthodox Jewish home filled with true "Yiddishkeit," along with five brothers Fishi, Benjamin, Bendi, Beresh, Smilku, my name was Yankele, later known as Alex. Our only sister Rosalyn (Rajziko) was the last and seventh child, and I was the sixth and last son. Our maternal Grandparents on mother's side lived with us, and mother's brother Yosef and his family lived close by in our village. Most of the other uncles, aunts, brothers and sisters on both sides had immigrated to America. Some other boys lived with us because they worked for our father, first as apprentices then as tailors in his tailor shop. The boys that worked for us were just like part of our family. We lived together and got along quite well in spite of so many of us being cooped up in small rooms without electricity, running water or gas. We even felt comfortable in our tiny home what today, especially in America, would be considered very cramped, below poverty quarters.

We lived in a small village called Palonok near the city of Munkach in the Carpathian Mountainous region of

Czechoslovakia (also known as Sub-Carpathian, Ruthenia), which was annexed by Hungary in 1940 when I was almost 12 years old. It is now part of the Ukraine. Our area used to be part of the Austrian-Hungarian Empire, before World War I. It was located between Czechoslovakia, Hungary, Romania, Poland, Ukraine and Russia. The Carpathian Mountain area was remote and very backwards by American standards, and even to the then European standards. We lived in a very small mud-block like house that faced a cobblestone, unpaved Main Street. No one owned a car in our village that I can remember, but a few of the people, the so-called middle class, had a horse and buggy which sustained them or some people owned a horse to ride to and from the adjoining villages or towns we also owned a cow to provide milk for the family, our Grandfather who lived with us, made his livelihood with a horse and buggy. The weather was kind of rough in our area during the summer and very miserably cold in the winter, snow fell early fall and stayed till late spring. The river froze about a foot thick , we could skate on it and in spring cut the ice up to be used all summer to keep the food from spoiling as we had no refrigerators.

Our father had a strong personality and was the typical ruler as most fathers were in those days, the boss of the house. However his love and devotion for his wife, our mother Etuko, his children, our grandparents, our employees (as well as the rest of the family) was always very apparent. His pride for his family showed in his eyes. All of us children took it for granted that our Father and Mother knew how much we loved and appreciated them. I have thought and regretted a million times that I can't recall if I ever told our parents how much I truly loved and appreciated them. I wish they could have survived and I would be able to tell them how much.

Father was very strict with us his children, yet he always taught and gave us the option to think for ourselves. For instance, while most of the religious Jewish boys in our village wore short hair with "payees," long side locks, he permitted us to grow our hair long and didn't force us to wear payees. We felt very proud to be given this privilege. Father also did not make us attend synagogue services every morning and evening, as a lot of our Orthodox Jewish friends and other Orthodox Jewish children in our village were required to do. However, in other ways, he was very insistent especially when it came to Sabbath observance. He implored not only his family, but also his employees it was a must to attend synagogue services every Friday evening and Saturday morning (for the Sabbath) as well as and all other Jewish Holy days. He not only saw to it that we kept the Sabbath holy, but we also had to keep a very strict kosher home. We also observed all of the orthodox customs and rituals of our faith and tradition. All Jewish holidays were kept and abided by according to "Halacha," Jewish Law just as it was practiced by our fore fathers. Father was the kind of man all boys needed as an example even today and, especially in those days. I am sure many boys growing up would have benefited from him even today. When he spoke to us, we had to listen carefully as we knew he never repeated himself, and he meant what he said! Just as any other children, we did not know how to fully appreciate him. Now, in our later years, we realize how very fortunate we were to have had him as our father. He was also respected amongst the Christian neighbors and the community in general. He was well known as a fine custom tailor. Most of the officers in the military Bastion overlooking our village had their clothing altered by him.

Actually, my father was known to be the best tailor in the entire area. He specialized in quality customized and personalized tailoring, hand sewn stitch by stitch they were truly hand-made suits. In fact his reputation as a good tailor was known in the whole Carpathian Region. People came from far away to have their clothing custom made by him. He had gotten his training in Vienna, Austria. In those days the best tailored clothing in the world was made in Vienna, Austria. He was well respected by all who knew him. He never failed to help someone in need and never believed himself to be superior to anyone. He enjoyed his work very much, almost as much as he enjoyed his family. When we were older we found out that our father had a son by a short, previous marriage that was amicably annulled after a couple of weeks. Because the matchmaker deceived them, he had no idea that he fathered a son till he was married to our mother. Our half brother did not live with us and we hardly knew him. Unfortunately, he died the day of liberation in Bergen Belsen where our sister Rosalyn saw him the day before she was liberated by the British Army. He died of Typhoid.

Our mother, on the other hand, was quite different from our father. She was affectionately called Etuko, and she was the love and envy of everyone! The only way to describe her was as a true angel on two feet sent from heaven. She was never upset to raise her voice, or get mad at us or anyone else. She radiated love to each of us and everyone around her. Above all she always had a smile. Like father (but even more-so) she was very proud of her large family. She not only loved us and her relatives' extended family, but also the employees who worked for and lived with us. She treated them as if they were her own family. She also took care of her elderly parents our precious grandparents, with a grateful and giving heart. Although she was always busy with her large and extended family she always had time in her quiet way to help beggars, strangers, even Gypsies, and anyone else who passed through our village; or for that matter anyone that needed a meal or came to her for help. She also taught us to love each other and to obey our elders. She especially emphasized respect for our father, our grandparents, and other elders. She taught us to respect each other as well as our neighbors and relatives or anyone we came into contact with.

Many of our friends and neighbors' kids loved to come over on Sabbath after the synagogue and they had their Sabbath meal at our home, because they loved our mother's scrumptious desserts so very much, for some reason they seemed to enjoy it more than their own Mother's desserts. Afterward, they would sing with us "Zemiros," ritual songs of appreciation for the blessings the Almighty bestowed on us. Every Sabbath we felt the joyous melodies seemed to ascend to heaven to uplift us.

Most of the time we could not afford to purchase many of the foods we wanted or needed for our large family at the store or market, so we grew a lot of our basic necessities in our small garden which produced most of the fruits and vegetables that we ate. On about one acre we also had a large apple, plum, cherry, peach, and a large walnut tree. We also grew all kinds of vegetables, such as carrots, cucumbers, corn, beans cabbage, etc. We housed a few chickens, and often had one or two ducks and geese which mother "stuffed" to fatten them up. We also had a cow for milk. We only bought the absolute essential necessities that we could afford and needed to sustain us. Mother was always canning cucumbers and beets, and making preserves during fall season to help feed our large family for the long cold, hard winter months, which lasted far too long in our mountainous area from early fall to late spring.

Just like most Jewish families then, were also too poor to buy toys or other games, but this was acceptable we did not know better because we always were able to feel satisfied and stimulated from our Jewish education in "Cheder" (Hebrew school) as well as our public school and especially the caring and guidance we got from our parents and grandparents. We didn't have any type of appliances, including electric or gas stove, no washing machines, dryers, no running water, no bathrooms, or showers, but we had outhouses and a hand dug water well.

Our synagogue had a communal bath ("Mikva") where we went to bathe ("cleuse") for our Sabbath. Mother had a helper or a maid to assist her. Mother milked the cow and gathered eggs every day. Mother's hands were never idle. Her love, compassion and non-biased judgmental treatment of others taught us to respect and care for people from all walks of life. As a result I never looked down on or discriminate against people because of their nationality, religion, sex, race, background, wealth or lack of it. To us, all people were equally good and we appreciated everyone. The love and security we received from our parents, grandparents and each other helped us to survive the horrors we had to endure in the Holocaust; as well as tremendously benefiting us later in our adult lives. Fortunately, all brothers and our sister are still living.

Every time I recollect about our very tiny home, to us at that time it appeared adequate. However it was below poverty level especially by American standards; I only remember how love abounded in our home. Even with numerous family members and several employees living with us, who made it well over a dozen, we didn't even feel crowded for meals or sleep. The main house which was also the business and cutting shop was not made of brick or stone, but hand made blocks made from mud, horse manure and straw. There was an earthen floor as most homes in our village had at that time. There were no frills in our home as only the very few rich people of our village or in the city had. Yet, we still felt that our home was our castle. Mother had a talent for not only sumptuous cooking but making everything we needed for our house including quilts, pillows, bed covers, and other beautiful things. She was tireless and this was most evident as you looked around our home. She even plucked the feathers from our stuffed geese and made thick quilts and plump pillows for our beds; she even managed to make them bright and pretty. The few curtains we had were sewn by her. She had a gift for making everyone who entered our home feel welcome and at-home. She showed real kindness and warmth to all of our friends and the employees. She never complained about the extra long hours of work that was bestowed on her. In fact, she never gave the appearance that she was working at all and her jovial disposition permeated the whole house.

Just like most people in those days, Mother also baked most of the bread eaten in our home, especially the "challahs" (Sabbath bread), which were served for Friday Evening Sabbath as well as on the Holy days. She did her daily cooking on a wood-fired stove using the largest pots/vessels that she could find and cooked for two or three days at a time, especially lunches which were our main meals of the day. She fed from thirteen to twenty people three times a day most of the time. Breakfast and lunch were our heaviest meals; it was believed to be needed for the hard physical work we did. Supper was the lightest because we had finished work for the day. Potatoes and beans were the mainstay for each meal with other vegetables like cucumbers, radishes, cabbage and corn (whichever were in season) were added to give variety and taste to our meal. The luscious fruits (abounded in the fall from our fruit trees) supplied mother with the means of making the desserts for which she was famous. Her pastries, especially the apple, peach, pear, nut, cherry or other pies, were the envy of every neighbor, especially the boys.

Philip and Bernie, the first and third sons, in certain ways were much like Father. They liked to work in the tailor shop as Father did. Ben, who was the second son, was learning to be a businessman in the city. Bernie, was talented and he also learned to play a mandolin, he provided our music to sing or dance to during the week in the evening. He also played the Balalaika, a Russian instrument much like a mandolin or Banjo. Sometimes when he played we danced with our sister, Rosalyn, Mother and others. One of us, especially the older boys, would pick Rosalyn up and dance with her and then pass her to another brother to be his partner. She squealed with delight and felt very important. We felt like she was a doll; her face would light up and she would have a cherubic look. Our parents, grandparents (when they were still alive), and even Dads workers, who were just like part of the family, shared our happiness and so did other friends and neighbors especially on Sabbath night.

Our sister Rosalyn was the youngest child and the only daughter, after six boys, to our parents. She was the apple of our parents' and our eyes. All of us brothers adored and cherished her too. We placed her on a pedestal and would do anything for her. She was a true joy to behold. Not only was she a beautiful and a lovable girl but she was also very well mannered. Her sunny disposition somewhat resembled that of our Mother's.

She was tall and very smart for her age and was the only one of us (except for Fishi, the eldest) to go to the famous Hebrew Polgary Gymnasium School in the adjoining city of Munkach. There were exceptionally fine teachers that taught there, and kids came from all over the world to attend this fine school.

One evening Rosalyn and I had to get seltzer water to mix with the wine for Sabbath. It was in the winter and because of all the snow was on the ground she did not want to go alone. We followed the same familiar route that we traveled by bike to the gymnasium. We were always frightened when evening fell as we passed the cemetery because sometimes boys would jump from dark places around the cemetery and shout at us with funny noises. They laughed at us as they saw how frightened we were. After they scared us, they would run away laughing even harder.

Our home and our village were just below a very large man-made mountain Bastion which was a large military base. According to today's standard of living in America, we would have been considered way below poverty level, but that was not the case then, not in our Village anyway. There we were considered "Middle Class." We were a happy old fashioned family blessed with hard work and good values, but most of all we had devoted loving parents, Grandparents family and friends. I fondly remember our wonderful maternal grandparents who were part of our childhood's everyday life. They were very jovial and loved by each of us as well as others who were lucky enough to be in contact with them. Even though they had endured a lot of hardships and sickness we never heard them complain. We felt very fortunate to have them live with us. I was very young when my mothers parents died, but I remember them very affectionately. Grandmother was slender and beautiful in every way. Our grandfather was a true "Jewish Zeyde," grandfather, with a long gray beard. I remember him caring for his horse & buggy which was his livelihood, and most of all, caring for and when ever possible spending time with his grandchildren. Our grandfather was a very pious man who attended religious in the village synagogue every morning, evening Sabbath and Holidays.

Our village was called Palanok, while we were under and part of the Czech Republic regime. Many times I used to sit and gave at the large man made bastion and at the majestic mountains, some not too distant that overlooked our village.

When I was eleven years old, our democratic country of Czechoslovakia was carved up. First, the Allies permitted Sudetenland, part of Czechoslovakia to be annexed by Germany; then the part where we lived, Carpathia, was annexed by Hungary when they joined and collaborated with the Nazi Germany. The name of our region was changed by the Hungarians from Carpathian Russia to Carpat-Alja; and our village became Va'r Pola'nko.

After that, Czechoslovakia and our lives would never be the same again. Even though Czechoslovakia was the first genuine Democratic country in Europe, patterned after the American Democratic System. Only later did we appreciate democracy that it was truly a great place to live that time in history. After the Hungarian annexation of our area, true democracy, freedom and our contentment had sadly been lost. Czechoslovakia could have become similar to the United States and Europe, where different ethnic and religious groups lived congenially, and got along well with each other. While there were ethnic and religious differences, there was no noticeable hate or incidence of strife. Along with Hungary taking our area over our lives were shattered for a long time and for most it was the beginning of the end.

Only a few hundred people lived in our village which was one of many small villages close to and adjoining the town of Mukachevo, which had maybe 50,000 people or better known later under Hungary as Munkach. The region that made up our area, especially the adjoining city of Munkach was filled with a majority of very religious pious Jews, known as Chasidim. Chasidics are followers and true believers of the Torah, our bible given to us through Moses, and they are the most pristine followers of the old Hebrew text God's teachings that rules and guides their everyday life. Munkach had many coal mines nearby, but the outlying area consisted of mostly farming, mining and logging timber for export there were also many farming fields around the mountains, as well as growing luscious grapes for the winery. Our village was bordered by many other villages; such as Davidkev, Inter-shlos, Klicherke, Lavik, and many other small villages mostly involved in farming, mining, logging and cattle raising. It was also close to the cities of Uzhgorod and Beregsaz, just to name a few cities in Carpathian. Mukachevo was then one of the largest towns in our area and real close to us and adjoining our village. There was also a large military base between our village and before you got to the city's downtown area. In addition to the military base on the man made mountain (or bastion) overlooking our village.

Our village adjoined almost half of this "large man-made mountain military bastion" which had been built by the Ottoman Empire and was supposedly used to defeat Napoleon and the French Imperial Army. This huge man-made mountain had a castle like military fortress on the top. This fortress was also used as a bastion by and for the Austria-Hungarian Army before World War I. The area of my birth place also became a training round and military base for the Czech Army. Then when the Carpathian Region was annexed by Hungary it became a training ground once again for the Hungarians until it was taken over by the German Army who also used it as a military base. The Munkach military base and our bastion was used by Germany for a military training base for the purpose to attack Russia, Poland, Romania, Lithuania, etc. Legend has it that this was where Napoleon met one of his worst defeats. When we were kids to us it truly resembled a gigantic mountain. The center of the mountain contained not only the military headquarters, it also has a hollow core, where it was rumored that in previous wars for punishment enemy soldiers were beaten, tortured and then thrown to their deaths in the well, plummeting down several hundred feet to a stream which bodies eventually ended in the Latorca River.

Speaking for so many who can't, our thoughts and dreams as children about this Bastion were filled with scary and ghostly stories. Unfortunately for us Jews these dreams turned into nightmares and these nightmares spread throughout our village as war seemed imminent. By February 3, 1942, rumors were rampant as to what was going on in Nazi Germany's occupied Poland where it was said that Jews were being murdered by the thousands or sent to concentration or extermination camps. However, the towns big Munkacher Rabbi was against the Jews going to Israel because he felt that Israel was a Zionistic state and not a religious one, that Meshiach (Messiah) will come, and it was up to the Almighty to deliver us to our Holy land. We also found out that England, North and South America or other countries did not let Jews into their country, so we had no choice but to stay together as a family and hope for a miracle: that Nazi Germany would be soon defeated. As a result of the rumors, children and youth were urged to stay away from the military mountain or wherever the soldiers were hanging out. We have also heard stories of muggings, rapes, and robberies that occurred, especially against Jews at or around the mountain as well as on the way to the city where soldiers partied. These horrendous activities also occurred at our village and others that surrounded it. This was good enough reason to stay away from the famous mountain and not to walk to the city alone especially at night. The age of the mountain alone was a deterrent to keep us away. After all, it was a man-made bastion before there was earth moving equipment or other ways to compact the dirt. Our parents were afraid that if an earthquake, tornado or torrential down pour would come, the old buildings on the man-made mountain would collapse, roll down and kill everyone in them and us nearby.

To reach the base of the structure, one had to ascend through our village then by way of a snake-like, brick paved road that wound, twisted and turned until you got to the top. Grapes, muscadines, cherries, and other fruit grew on the side of the mountain and along the curving road. Fruit trees, and especially grapes for wine seemed to grow better not only along the path, but all around the mountain. These luscious fruit trees made it very hard for us kids to stay away. Some of the more daring youth would sneak and pick the "forbidden fruit," most often in the fall late at night as it was not easy to be seen. But you had to be very careful, because it was steep, not to fall and get hurt, or to be caught by the owners.

Before fascism took over our area because the large military base was between our villages on the road to the City, it brought many military people, especially the officers, into our Father's tailor shop. Many of the Jewish people in our area were sheepherders, fruit growers, honey and wine makers (from bees); as well as, merchants working with horses and buggies. Our surrounding mountain area was a treasure for ore, coal, and other minerals. The flat land especially along the river was also a fertile valley for food crops. Many countries desired or occupied the region at times: including, Ottoman Empire Turkey, Austria, Hungary, Russia, Germany, and others. There were also wood-cutting mills, craftsmen and mill workers. It was fitting that this symbol of my birthplace would come to represent the many bad and good things that happened to me in my early as well as later years in life. The many trials, tribulations, joys, sufferings, hiding, resurfacing, and entrapment; not to mention the feelings of lost love, then, fortunately being loved again by many people, especially early in my life by my parents, then being blessed with a wonderful wife and four children, but unfortunately loosing my parents who were murdered in the holocaust, then loosing my son in a farming accident then loosing my beloved wife to a rape murderer after twenty five years of blissful marriage.

In the late 1930's and early 1940's (when I was a youngster) times were very hard economically in our area, as it also was throughout Europe and indeed in the rest of the world. Daily living became a strain on all of us as well as the villagers, yet with all of the economic problems there seemed to be a feeling of closeness, cooperation, caring, and belonging. There was great cooperation, caring not only from our close family but from one family to another. This camaraderie was prevalent among all of the neighbors regardless of religious, ethnic, or political differences. There was contentment under the Czech democratic regime in our village, especially amongst the Jewish people. All the Jewish children attended "Cheder," Hebrew School and synagogue whenever possible we especially looked out for each other.

The Jewish families in our area were very close; we shared not only on inherent bond, but we had strong traditional ties through our synagogue and its reveres Rabbis. We also abided by the same laws pertaining to our food which was all strictly kosher and inspected by the Rabbi or Schoichet. Another aspect that unified us was our common languages: Yiddish, which was what we spoke at home and Hebrew which we learned in Hebrew school when we prayed and studied our bible.

Our popular Czech leaders, President Thomas Garik Masarik and Vice President Benesh, seemed to be liked and respected by everyone in our country, as well as Europe, and the world community in general. President Masarik showed concern for all segments of the population. Like in other parts of the world, we had cities, towns, and villages where some people were better off than others, but this is to be expected. Even with the economic differences, we were a small friendly village that got along with other villagers, as well as the adjoining villagers and townspeople. Most of our neighbors were boot-makers, tailors, farmers, bakers, miners, lumberman, laborers, or horse traders. Neighbors shared and bartered or traded food and clothing with each other. Food or craft gifts were given at weddings or when new babies arrived and moral support was given when families lost loved ones. Children gathered together to play games, especially soccer (which we called football) whenever we could get a real ball. Without a real ball we would have to make a somewhat round ball from old rags tied together with a string. In our time and area, "football" was the only sport played.

Our village of Polanok and adjoining villages were mostly made up of many Shwaaben (who were of German descent), some in the adjoining villages and towns had Hungarians, mostly Ruskie, Russians, Jews and a few Czechs or Slovaks. We even had a few gypsies who moved in and out of our area, but they never actually settled in. As children we were a little in awe and yet afraid of the gypsies (maybe of being kidnapped), so as kids we stayed away from them. There was one other Schwaben village nearby; however, most of the other surrounding smaller villages seemed to be mostly Ruskie or Sub-Carpathian Ruthenia speaking. For most of the people, farming or mining was their livelihood. They worked hard six days a week and rested on the Sabbath or Sunday. They would grow enough food on their farms or back yard for their own consumption and sell what was left or barter to other villagers or town people. In turn, products that they needed could be bartered for what they grew. Once or twice a week they would take what they grew or made to the main market in the center of Munkach to sell for cash or swap for other necessities. The Jews made up between 10 and 15 percent of the area population overall, but as much as 40 to 60 percent of the adjoining town of Munkach's population, some of whom were extremely religious.

My family was one of the fifty or so observant Jewish families in our village (there were a few more Jews in the adjoining villages) who belonged to our Synagogue. We were very close to everyone even though we were not-as-ultra-orthodox (very religious) as most of the Jewish families in our area. We were all within walking distance of each other and the synagogue.

We lived together, worked together, and attended synagogue together. Most of the people attended services every day, in the morning and evening. There was little time for anything else, yet our lives were very full, and we enjoyed being together. There was no automation in those days; everything had to be done by hand. There were no telephones, radios, televisions and most homes including ours had no electricity until the last few years or running water. Everyone learned to become handy at taking care doing things for themselves.

Going to "Cheder" Hebrew School was not fun to me. I was not a good student of the Alef-Bet-Gimel-Dalet (the Hebrew ABC's). The "Lerer" or Hebrew teacher was very strict and mean, especially to me. I got my share of beatings from him that left indelible scars on me, but I did not dare tell Father about it because he would have given me more of a shellacking for being a bad boy!

I looked up to each of my five older brothers. In their own way they were my champions. I felt that they each were about ten feet tall. Father tried to train us in his trade and he hoped we would become good tailors one day. He dreamed we would follow in his footsteps and become very famous tailors just like him. He also hoped we would take over the business he built up or just plain succeed where ever we go. He wanted, as most European fathers did, for his sons to be in the business with him. Back then a tailor was a good wage earner. It was good that he had so many other dependable men working for him who were just like family, but he still dreamt of giving apprenticeship to his own "flesh and blood." When each son reached a certain age he had to work and help in the tailor shop. Father felt that this would give each son a feel of the profession; not to mention the fact that he also needed the help. The younger sons, usually me and Sam who was a couple of years older, also helped with chores in the shop and at home. I remember vaguely when, at five years old, I was expected to be in the shop by 5 or 6 AM. It was y responsibility to light the fire under the coal and to keep it going by blowing air at it with my mouth, so that the irons could be heated and ready for pressing the garments by the time the tailors needed the irons hot. It was difficult for a five year old to get the fire started because of the smoke and soot to keep it going because the coal was in large chunks and fresh out of the coal mines, no doubt black soot went into our lungs which were not far away from our home. Sam and I also had to chip wood and bring it in the house to be used by mother in the kitchen for cooking and heating the house. Sometimes my older brothers Philip, Ben, Bernie, or Bill, would be asked to help cut and split the wood which was then stacked in a shack adjoining our home and was to be taken into the house by Sam or me, as needed since we were the youngest boys. As we grew older our jobs changed.

The front part of our home was also used by our father for the main tailor fitting and cutting shop. There were cloth samples, patterns, and rolls of fabric stored there so that customers could pick out their choice of fabric for us to make their suits. There was a cutting table and one foot paddling sewing machine. The rest of the foot-pedaled sewing machines, ironing tables, and work place, were in a back building next to the hay shack and where the cow and horse were housed. When the shop closed at the end of each day, the cutting tables were filled with straw opened up and became our beds. This arrangement was a very practical solution for our small home as it gave us the extra needed space for the multitude that lived in it. I remember the fun I used to have when I was allowed to sleep in the back bungalow where the older boys slept. I fondly remember spending many happy hours in the bungalow listening to my older brothers telling stories. I was too young to participate so I do not remember any of the stories. Naturally just like normal stories in those days, they centered on girls, and playing football (soccer). Many times I slept on top of haystacks in that building with a cousin Burnie Lebovitz or Jonchi, a Schwabish boy from across the street; things changes drastically when anti-Jewish laws were enacted life became more and more difficult for us and Jonchi became first a Hitler Youth then an SS officer.

As our second oldest brother Ben grew up, he developed an interest in a field other than that of a tailor. First he worked in the adjoining city of Munkach in a cloth store he then decided he wanted to be a butcher, along with out Uncle Yosef. They slaughtered cattle at night in the back of our house in the barn where our cow was next to the tailor shop. They prepared the meat according to Kashrut law, which helped our neighbors, as well as people in the adjoining city obtain kosher meat which was banned. They were supervised by a "Shoichet," a certified Jewish slaughterer who acted as a Kashrut observer. Uncle Yosef and his family lived near us in our village. By then it was against the law by the Fascist Hungarian regime to sell or make the meat kosher. Our Father was very upset about this, he would say "I can not understand why they won't allow us to kosher our meat; after all it's a known fact that the meat is cleaner and healthier than non-kosher meat." When meat is koshered even the fat and veins are removed from the meat. It was really just another Hungarian Fascist anti-Semitic law to make our lives more difficult. Uncle Yosef and Ben would work till very late night or early morning skinning the cattle, cutting out the veins, weighing and cutting up the meat packaging to fill the orders to be delivered, not only to out villages, but to the city of Munkach adjoining villages. All the while they did the butchering other family members watched out for the police. They made sure that they and the Shoichet were safe because he observed to make sure that the meat was prepared according to the Kashrut Law. They would hang the slaughtered cattle in the barn next to our tailor shop where our cattle was so the blood would drain out to the back.

When Ben and Uncle Josef were finished, the Shochet inspected the meat again and approved the front section as kosher. Only the front of the cattle is considered to be kosher. The watchers would continue to look out for police as Uncle Yosef and Ben placed the cut up and packaged kosher meat onto a horse drawn wagon cover it to disguise it, to be taken into the city. They were proud that they could distribute the kosher meat to the Jewish people for their Sabbath meal even though this was a precarious act. The Fascist police would arrest, punish or deport them if they were caught. Most Jewish families in our area were observant Jews who kept strict kosher kitchens like ours. Mostly vegetables were eaten during the week and only on special occasions (if they could afford it) such as the Sabbath or holidays would they eat kosher chicken or beef. To the Jewish people of our area the Sabbath was truly a holy day, not just a holiday.

When I was about eleven years old, I was considered strong and healthy for my age. I was permitted to help Uncle Yosef and Ben with their meat deliveries to the village on foot or to the city by bicycle. We waited for darkness each Thursday night. Usually about midnight, or very early Friday morning, I loaded my bike up with meat in the front and in the back, as well as the knapsack on my back. I made the deliveries in the city early in the morning so that the Jewish people would have their meat fresh and in time to prepare for their precious holy Sabbath meal. Obviously, I was frightened and anxious, but I wanted to help them in any way I could. Many times I would also deliver meat when I took our sister Rosalyn to the city's Hebrew school gymnasium.

Early on Thursday morning you could see the local farmers passing our home from many villages to take their items to where everyone gathered in the center of the city which was like an open business market to sell or swap their vegetables, chickens, eggs, and other animals, and fruits during the season for other items that they needed or could not grow like cloth, clothing, shoes, etc. The carts and wagons hauled chickens, ducks, and geese; as well as vegetables and fruit. Many times a farmer had to walk many kilometers or take an animal or self drawn cart from one village to another (or to the city) to make his trade or sale. We were always excited when Father was able to make a swap for something delicious to eat that week, especially for Sabbath. Father often traded tailoring for food items, especially when the Nazis took over.

Winters in Eastern Europe especially in our mountainous area are known for their extreme cold and snow but the close by mountain range in our area seemed to be the coldest and snow and ice stayed the longest. The snow that came down early in the winter months stayed on the ground until spring. The Laturca River that ran through our village was only a few hundred yards from our home. The river would always freeze over a foot thick in the winter. When this happened we were happy because we would skate on the ice with our shoes. Since we could not afford ice skates, we still managed to slide across the ice on our worn out shoes. Sometimes we tried creating makeshift skates. Ice skating as well as throwing snow at each other or making a large snow man was always the highlight of our long cold winter months. Everyone joined in, even Rosalyn who was only a little girl. At first she always fell on the ice, but later she became just as good as we were. Of course, in the summer when it was really warm, and if we had time we would swim in the Laturca River.

Several of the villagers made a business during the late winter or early spring of cutting the ice from the river into large squares, storing it in underground basements or storage areas and selling it in summer months during warm weather. There were no refrigerators in our area in those days, for keeping milk or meat fresh, or any other foods from spoiling. We used ice for storing meats and other foods, such as butter, cream, and milk, for the spring and summer months. They would cut enough ice for most peoples use and stored it in underground storage areas. Some of the affluent villagers had basements or special cellars to keep their ice stored there. This permitted them to have some ice during the entire summer when they needed it because mother cooked in large pots and food had to last several days.

There was very little electricity available in our area at that time. When I was 11 years old we finally had electricity in the front of our home for use in the tailor shop, where the cutting and the selling was done. This is where Mother, Dad, Rosalyn and I lived. We did not have any electricity in the tailor work shop where the sewing, ironing and other work was done; not in the building where the boys slept. Like most people, at night we used kerosene lamps or candles for light until 1941 or 1942.

We also had a hand dug water well because there was no piped or city water system in our area. This of course meant no showers or bathrooms we had outhouses and used buckets of water in a tub to bathe with. (Remarkably, when I visited the area (there is now city water) but 50 years later the same well was still there.) We drew the water up in a bucket and filled pails to carry the water into the house. Our parents gave Sam and me the task of making sure there was plenty of water for mothers cooking in the house at all times. Though we were still young, we skillfully drew water from the well and carried the heavy buckets to the house. Sometimes a goose or rooster would run to attack me and scare the wits out of me and I would spill the water. My older brothers or employees would always get a kick out of it and laugh, which made me upset. I was angry at the goose for scaring me and at my older brothers or others for laughing at me but that was life then.

On the top of and between the tailor work shop in the back, next to the cow and horse barn, was the hay storage area. Some of us boys would sleep there, on top of the hay, especially in the warm full summer months. We did not have mattresses or blankets, as we know today only some handmade quilts in our home. That was something I always looked forward to because we could stay awake longer and "kibitz," talk nonsense with my buddies. I felt a little older each time I could join the older boys, and there was always room on the haystacks for my friends, cousins, (as well as my close cousin, Bumy, Uncle Yosef's son), and other Jewish or non-Jewish friends like Jonchi from across the street who later became an SS Obersturm fuhrer.

In those days there was very little public school teaching in our area several age groups were bunched together in a small building. To us, it seemed as though it was a long way to walk to and from school, and it was practically in the next village the main reason it became bad or long for us because

23

we had to walk past a Catholic Church, where on occasion (especially after the annexation of our area by Fascist Hungary) the Catholic boys would attack us and accuse us of killing their Christ, even though the Priest (who was a friend of our fathers') tried to stop them.

When we got to the school, the children of all ages were grouped together because there were just a few classroom and teachers. The school was in a rundown building with a very small backyard for a playing field. We also attended Hebrew school every day late in the afternoon and Sundays, to learn the Hebrew alphabet and prayers, but I could not learn the meanings. The Rabbi, as well as the Hebrew teacher were very strict and sometimes mean. The "Lerers" (teachers) taught us Hebrew and most of all to follow the strict Orthodox teachings of the original Torah (Bible). We also were taught to obey and respect the religious laws and principles of Judaism. We were taught that God and his commandments came before everyone or anything. This was hard for me to accept it as I felt that my parents and family should come first. As I grew older, without my parents, whom I miss terribly even to this day, I came to realize that the teachers and the Rabbi were correct on many points and that God, indeed, came first. After all He works in mysterious ways and none of us are able to fully understand or comprehend why certain events pleasant or unpleasant tragedies occur in our lives or what long range effects they have on us or the future generations.

Sabbath was the highlight of our week, and it entailed a lot of preparation, especially for our mother. The cooking, baking, and cleaning were done in advance as these were some of the restrictions on the Sabbath. The Sabbath was a very special time that was devoted to rest, prayers, and togetherness. As

Rosalyn matured, Mother helped her learn how to do all of the things that were to be expected of Jewish women in preparation of the Holy Sabbath.

We, the boys, on Friday afternoon, had to get cleaned up and ready for the Sabbath. We would first take our ritual bath (Mikva) in the synagogue on Friday afternoon, get dressed in our best clothing, our one set of decent clothes. All the boys would then leave with Father for the Synagogue as a family unit, especially for the Friday evening service when it was over. We returned home together for the festive Friday Eve Sabbath meal, and after we ate we sang Zemiros (religious songs) and thanked God after the meal. Early Saturday morning the entire family went to the synagogue for morning prayers which was then followed by Kiddush, which was sponsored most of the time by those in celebration of a wedding, Bar Mitzvah, when a boy becomes 13 years old or anniversary, or other reason for some sponsor to provide schnapps (a little vodka) and other sweets. Then we came home for a festive Sabbath lunch, which was our main meal of the week followed again by singing Zemiros where many times friends and neighbors, especially boys from the village joined us. After the supposed afternoon rest, we returned to the synagogue for Shala Shudith, and the late afternoon Mincha service which was followed by the evening Maariv prayers in the synagogue. Mother would be proud of us and the way we looked and acted. Supposedly our Sabbath rest prepared us for hard work the following week and we looked forward to the coming of Sabbath yet again.

Father, Mother and Rosalyn many times went for walks on the Sabbath afternoon. It was their special time together. Sometimes the boys sneaked away to play soccer at a field which was on the way to the city. As long as our elders did not know about it, then we came home. The elder boys all dressed up would walk to the city for the evening socializing around the city square or go to the movie house, where they tried to meet girls on dates.

For many years, our father was the Gabbai (overseer) of the Synagogue. He frequently led the congregation in prayers and song because he had such a good voice. Our Jewish community was so small that we could not afford to hire a Cantor or full time Rabbi. Of all the children, the two older sons, brothers Philip and Bernie, had the best voices and we loved it when they sang the prayers with our father. Later, Bernie was accepted in the famous Munkacher Cantorial School to study as a cantor. Some of the most famous cantors, such as Yoself Rosenblat and other world renowned cantors had studied there. Father was very proud that one of his sons was accepted and had a splendid voice, that he would someday potentially be a fine cantor.

During the week when the services in the synagogue were concluded, but especially on Sabbath, when our father would meet strangers or even beggars passing through our village he wanted to be sure that they would not go hungry. He insisted they should come home with us on any day, but especially for our Sabbath meal. He always invited strangers who needed food or companionship. Father extended the invitation without embarrassing them. He would say, "Mr. what ever your name is, my wife, Ettele, was expecting out of town guests, and she has prepared far too much food for us, and since they did not show up would you please honor us at our home and help us to eat the food?" They were glad to respond with a "Yes" because of mother's reputation she was such a great hostess and cook. We were blessed many times with strangers, especially for our Sabbath noon meals.

Our Sabbath meal was far different from our daily meals. On the Sabbath, we had what we thought a feast. There was sometimes real meat, like roast beef ribs or steak, when we could afford it, if not a duck, geese or chicken and almost every vegetable and fruit that Mother could think of and was able to get. Her desserts were the highlight and exquisite finishing touch of the fine meal. Mother's home made baked desserts were the delight of everyone who tastes them. Often our neighbors' kids would drop by after their own Sabbath meal, just to be tempted by these wonderfully delicious desserts. Boys of all ages, from mid teen to thirties who were our friends, especially liked to share in these scrumptious desserts. Most of them would invent excuses to leave their home early so that they could drop by our house. After our Sabbath meal was finished, we sang and they joined us in the ritual singing of Zemiros. Our singing was directed to the Almighty, and it was lively, joyous and full of love. Then we finished it with the Birchat Hamazon prayer, in which we thanked the Almighty for blessing us with the food from the Earth.

As far as sports games went, soccer was our favorite and really our only sport in those days. Some of the affluent in the city, such as doctors, etc., played tennis but we could not afford a racket or balls. All of us boys played soccer fairly well. Of course, we did not have proper equipment, such as soccer shoes, shin guards, uniforms or even a good soccer ball. I don't even know if there were many people in our area who could afford these items in those days. We tied the rags with strings and wound them round and round to make our "ball" hard, yet light and soft enough to stay round. Our goals were also homemade, like putting a cap or a rock the approximate width of a goal. For us, it was of course forbidden to play soccer on the Sabbath, so sometimes we slipped out of our village and went to the next town or village for a game. The only real soccer field was located close to our village just inside the next city. Sometimes the games were friendly and sometimes they were a little "too friendly" and someone would get hurt.

I remember once getting kicked very hard on the shin when we played against a German fascist group of Hitler youth boys. I could not tell my parents that I had been hurt playing soccer on the Sabbath, because I would have gotten us all in trouble. My leg swelled up badly and became infected and very painful. I could not walk on it. Finally after a few days, my Mother called a mid-wife, who also acted as a nurse, as we could not afford doctors. She placed some leaved and a poultice on my leg to draw out the infection. Slowly, but surely, the pain subsided. Years later, in England, I found after an x-ray was taken of the many injuries I had suffered in the camps that the soccer injury may have resulted in a broken leg. I was not sure because it had been broken at least once in the camps by either Kapo or an SS guard who loved to kick us in the shin. I probably suffered a broken leg then but could not let anyone know it in the Buna camp or I would have been sent to the Auschwitz gas chamber immediately.

As a young boy I also remember and affectionately recall a visit from the Weis family from Chicago, who had a bakery they lived across from us. I was names after their father when he passed away. When they came back from America to visit their brother and mother who still had a bakery and they brought their gorgeous seven or eight year old daughter, Janet with them. We were so glad to have visitors, especially from America. In the Jewish faith, especially among us Ashkenazi Jews, a person named his children after loved ones who have passed away to perpetuate the name. I was named after Janet's grandfather, the baker who passed away just before I was born, because they had no children. From the first moment I laid eyes on Janet, I fell in love with her because we had many boys in our family and they had no grandsons. After all puppy love is still love!

I remember she had the most beautiful, long hair that I had ever seen and wore it braided or in long curls. Her smile held so much joy for me and her smile stayed with me for many years, even through my worst ordeals in the camps at the hand of Hitler's Fascist torturers. I thought about her affectionate bright smile often in the extermination camps; she was one more reason that I fought as hard as I did for survival. I felt that if I could survive, then maybe someday I could join her in America. We would be reunited, live as in the fairy tales, happily ever after. We were inseparable the entire time she and her family visited our area. I felt that I had a friend and a true love for life. There was nothing that we couldn't share. She ate frequently at our home for the duration of their stay and her parents took me with them everywhere.

Her American family was very wealthy by our standards and their wealth was noticed wherever they went. I was told by them that if I could ever get to America I was invited to stay with them. But as most at that time, I could only wish for this one. The dream eventually came true to a point. A few years after being liberated in Buchenwald and the war was over, when I finally arrived in America, I tried to contact her through her uncle who was in touch with my brothers. She was one of the reasons that I got a job with my friend Jerry Hornstein in Chicago as a contact lens specialist. Her parents, however, made it impossible for me to get together with her. I could only see her from a distance because her family did not want her to become friendly or associated with a penniless refugee.

After many calls I found out where they lived. I sort of invited myself over one Saturday morning. After waiting for her until noon in an unwelcome home, I left and waited on the corner for her to return. When she got off the bus, my heart and eyes lit up. She was tall and beautiful, just as I had imagined her to be all those years. We did not speak nor did she know who this guy was standing on the corner. Later, I found out that Janet was dating someone seriously so I had to get on with my life and wished her well. I wanted to join the US Army because the Korean War had just broken out. From then on I was left with only my fond memories of her but I never saw her again.

Now back to my childhood memories. The political atmosphere in Europe was changing fast newspapers and industrialists in Germany were backing a convicted criminal Nazi named Adolph Hitler who openly boasted his ideals to Eliminate the Jewish people and conquer the world to create a 1,000 year German Reich that will control the entire world.

These, and many more childhood memories only came to the surface after many years of fighting to unravel my past. The trauma of the camps lurked into my childhood memories like cancer cells invading what was healthy and good. Never again would I experience the same kind of complete joy no matter how austere life we led as I had in my parents' home with my entire unified family before the Second World War. Hitler and his cohorts robbed me of my youth, my education, and many wonderful memories just as he robbed me of many happy years with my parents, grandparents, all my aunts, uncles, cousins, and friends that remained in Europe from my childhood we lost our beloved parents and most relatives. My five brothers, one sister and I were very fortunate; we were the only family of seven siblings to have survived the Holocaust. We were truly blessed - all of my mother's children survived. In fact almost all my relatives, all my Aunts and Uncles on my Father's and Mother's side and most cousins, and close friends that stayed in Europe were exterminated in the concentration camps. Most families would have considered themselves lucky to have one or two survivors, let alone seven children. Only now, fifty years later, am I able to bring these memories to the surface to share them with others, recognizing how lucky we were, that so many of our family, brothers and sister, survived the Holocaust in spite of the untold suffering we endured. I mourn the cruel and unfortunate loss of so many innocent people at the hands of the Nazis.

Yes, our family roots were in our village for centuries and I still struggle with the notion that our neighbors became enthusiastic Nazis and willing killers. They consciously chose to be participants in Hitler's conquest to dominate Europe and indeed the world by killing first all of the Jews as well as others that did not go along with their Fascists ideals, even if we were their neighbors, friends, and fellow man. The only thing that mattered was that they considered themselves superior people. The Nazis unleashed their Satanic forces which engulfed most of Europe pronouncing Irrevocable sentence of death upon millions and millions of innocent people by reason of status of birth alone then on anyone that stood in their way from achieving complete and total control of body and mind.

Not all are guilty, but we all bear responsibility for not stopping these boisterous extremists before it was too late for millions upon millions of innocent people as well as themselves.

Chapter 2: A Changing Village

I was still an innocent young boy in our Carpathian mountainous region; we lived in the small backward village of Polanok, Czechoslovakia. Unfortunately, hell started breaking out for us when Czechoslovakia was carved up. Hungary joined up with Hitler's Nazi Germany in their fascist quest to take over the world. As a result our area was taken over by Hungary, which to me was a very traumatic day even though I was only eleven years old. They changed the name of our village immediately from Polanok to Va'r Pola'nko in Hungarian. Our area changed hands many times in the past. History tells us that one time our area was part of the Russian Empire, then Turkish Empire, Austro-Hungary, and I am sure others ruled our area. By 1940 many countries in Europe were in turmoil, even in our backward Carpathian Mountain region things were topsy-turvy.

At that time there remained in Europe a choice between a peaceful co-existence amongst people of different countries, languages, ethnic backgrounds, religion, or nationality, we had all kinds of people surrounding us, Ruskie, German Gypsies, Jews, Checks, Slovak, Hungarians. Our village and one adjoining village were mostly German, the others mostly

Ruskie, the adjoining city mostly Jewish. However, we got along well, but most people there were apathetic, as they are in many areas even now. Very few of the decent people cared or wanted to get involved to stop the extremists like Hitler and his Fascists cohorts in order to keep peace. Of course there were other religious leaders, like the Emperor of Japan, Mussolini of Italy, Stalin of Communist Russia and others.

Some of the older people of our village were aware of what was happening and told us not to worry that our region changed hands before many times. Before World War I our area was part of Austro-Hungary. After World War I it became Czechoslovakia. Even before World

War II broke out our area was annexed in 1940 by Hungary because they co-operated with Hitler in their war effort, then, in 1944 Germany stopped trusting anyone, so they took our area over from Hungary because the Germans felt that they were world's invincible master race and did not trust even their own Allies, such as the Hungarians, the French, the Italians, the Japanese, etc.

Our family lived in this area, whose culture and language was German, and in this home, a very substandard life for many generations as did most people, especially the Jews, most of them were very religious and the Sabbath to us was truly holy. In the nearby town of Munkach which adjoined our village, 55-60% of the population was Jewish, mostly very religious, strict Orthodox, pious and Sabbath observant. When I was eight years old our Father bought me for the first time a brand new pair of shoes at the Bata shoe store, but otherwise my clothes including shoes were hand-me-downs from my older brothers.

As the world knows now, after World War I, the countries of Europe, which included Germany, were trying to regain the economic and prestigious status they enjoyed prior to WWI, especially the Austro-Hungarian Royalty, (whose ranks declined during WWI) also the elite, and many of the wealthy industrialists were struggling to recover from World War I and they were not willing to give up control but life went on for us somehow. Times were hard for almost everyone throughout Europe, as well as in the western countries, and our area of Sub-Carpathian in Ruthenia was no exception, things were tough on us.

What the citizens of Germany or those new countries aligning with the Hitler's Fascist movement did not realize, and were not willing to accept, was that the entire world was in a depression experiencing unemployment problems and other hardships as well as work shortages, even Great Britain, the United States and other countries were not exempt from these hardships and its people suffered economic as well as work problems.

We heard that they set up as many as 50 camps throughout Germany supposed to exterminating enemies first the Communists then opposition surely followed, the Jehovah's Witnesses, social democrats or people who opposed the regime, then Jews.

Had the Germans not heard of the American Depression and suffering or they did not want to hear of it, or the collapse of Wall Street, the soup lines, or people in America committing suicide because even some of the wealthy people could not pay their bills and support their families? Most people were out of work and hard times were endured by most of the Americans, as well as other people throughout the world. However, Hitler and his right wing cohorts ceased the opportunity to arise hate in the German people who were nationalist anyway, espousing that they were the superior race, designated to rule the world, and any and all their problems were the fault of the Jewish or other minority people. Unfortunately, most German people were happy to get involved with Hitler, especially in the conquest of the world, most felt that any excuse is as good as another excuse for them to take over and rule the world.

Our elders, as well as others, did not concern themselves with this and chose to ignore the fact that in Germany's Hitler, their rising boisterous Nazi leader, who at first could not even hold onto the ranks of a corporal in the Army, blamed all problems and difficulties the German's were experiencing was the fault of others, especially the small minority Jewish population of less than 2%. We became their "under umglik," the cause of or blame for all their problems and for their misfortunes because we Jews were vulnerable, a small minority, in Germany, and we practiced a different religion, worked hard and achieved some respectable status, this just boosted the anti-Semitic theories.

Because of the rapid rise of the right wing elements, anti-Semitic was growing rampant, not only in Germany, but it caught on throughout the fascist aligned countries of Europe, our village, which was inhabited mostly by Schwaben, or German descendants. The Jews were also becoming the scapegoat for all that was wrong in Germany, as well as in our village and many other parts of Europe. We were not only blamed for all of the wrong in Germany's economy but also the people's own personal family problems. It was so convenient for the fascists to bring out in the open their anti-Semitic to blame for their shortcomings on the Jewish minority, not only to take away our power but also our possessions; because no one, especially the vast majority of freedom loving, but apathetic people paid little or no attention to the hate mongers in Germany and the Nazis threats throughout the world in general.

The political atmosphere in Europe was changing fast for all people and especially for us Jews. Suddenly newspapers in Germany were backing a convicted criminal, a fanatically little known person by the name of Adolph Hitler who wrote a hate-filled book called Mein Kampf. His book became very popular first amongst hate mongers and he was growing in importance, not only in Germany but in neighboring Austria where he was born, as well as, other German Allied Countries, even areas formerly occupied, ruled or settled by them, especially people who were of German descent.

Hitler quickly climbed the political ladder. He changed his stand from first being somewhat a left-wing rebel rouser, labor leader, or communist, to a serious right-wing "Nazi," a totally new phenomenon in the political arena. He used his passionate rhetoric first appealing to the bigots, in the beer halls of Germany, to instill hatred for the Jewish and other minority people in order to gain their complete support, strength and then solidify his popularity amongst all German people. His idea was to create a pure Aryan race, he espoused and preached openly "Deutschland über Alles--Germany over everything." As a result, most of the German people enthusiastically embraced his Fascist policies especially of hatred for the Jews, because he promised them that they could take away our homes, jobs, business, and all our possessions. This was the beginning of our demise because he gained by this many enthusiastic followers and the apathetic majority of good people did nothing.

Hitler was no different from other dictators. First he gained the leadership and loyalty of his closest people in the Nazi Party by recruiting and using innocent youth, as well as criminals, and anyone that was impressionable or easy to influence. He promoted his loyal followers rapidly within the fascist party to solidify his undisputed power and leadership position amongst the party members at first and later the entire German nation. Once Hitler gained power, he got rid of doubters through harassment and arrests, putting the opposition into Dachau and Buchenwald, the first of many concentration camps that were created. As a result he eliminated or had no opposition, and it appeared that no one had the guts or stood up against him or his Nazi philosophy. The making of a ruthless society was a natural result, which delighted him and his cohorts because, for the most part, the German people embraced the Nazi philosophy and Hitler's Fascist leadership with enthusiasm. Our area, even though it became part of Fascist Hungary, was no different once Hungary took control of our area from Czechoslovakia, the same thing happened, most of them embraced the Nazi or Hungarian Fascist philosophy, anti-Semitic grew rapidly and totally out of hand.

As the world has learned, Hitler, who was Austrian, could not advance in the German military ranks, so he jumped into the political arena. For a few years preceding his election, he used every possible moment to give speeches on street corners, beer halls, and youth clubs or to anyone who would listen. In these vicious speeches he ridiculed the German establishments, industrialists, businessmen, bureaucracy, capitalism, politicians and common decency of people that did not agree with his fascism. Above all he blamed the Jews, other minorities and the allies for all of Germany's problems. From street corners and beer halls to the civic halls, there was no speech that did not espouse vengeance against the allies, and hatred especially for the Jewish people everywhere, including America.

He convinced the German people of their superiority over everyone and anyone, even those Germans who were less intelligent, felt superior if they were of German descent. They became fervent followers of Hitler's diatribe; this resulted in the Jewish people becoming the scapegoats for all their problems. The Germans began a program of hate, barbarism and murder unprecedented in history. They implemented the systematic murder of millions of innocent people, the total destruction of European Jewry to make it "Judenrein." (free of Jews)

Even though Hitler never got a majority of votes in Germany because of disarray, there was suddenly the "Kristal Nacht," the crystal night of the broken glass, when Synagogues were burned and Jewish store windows were smashed. Soon he was appointed Chancellor. Anti-Semitism grew rampantly as soon as Hitler and his cohorts took command, and Jewish people found out quickly they had no jobs available for them. Many Jews attending college or the universities were expelled, thousands of highly trained professional people, musicians, teachers, scientist, doctors, and trained professionals found themselves without an income. They had to take a menial job, such as sweeping the streets, cleaning, any jobs that the Germans considered beneath them. These highly trained Jewish educators, doctors, lawyers, clergymen, businessmen, all were forced to immigrate from Germany or do menial jobs in order to be able to support themselves and their families. The Nazis followed that basic philosophy every where including our area which was taken over and ruled by Fascist Hungary.

A person was considered Jewish, and not a citizen of the area, even if their great grandparents were born there. It started first in Germany and then in other countries they conquered, or lived in, and even if their grandparents lived as Christians and

Germans or whatever Nationality. He espoused that if there was even just one drop of Jewish blood, several generations back, running through their veins, they were considered by them to be an undesirable and a Jew. We were ridiculed because hatred against Jews was rampant, and was spreading like the plague all over Germany and its Allied or occupied countries. Even young Jewish students were not spared, as they were not even permitted to attend most schools and universities to complete their studies.

Most of the Jewish people in Germany, and their Nazi controlled territories, who could tried to immigrate; but it was not easy. Hardly any country wanted to let the Jews in. This included Britain, Canada, America, and even South America.

At first when we heard about it we thought these persecutors or executions were false rumors and that our American relatives would not let them harm us or let them stop us from leaving for America to join them, but now we were confronted with similar problems we heard about as soon as our area was taken over by the Hungarian Fascist Regimes. We found out even if you had a visa to go to America, you, as a Jew, were not allowed to cross over any of the Fascist controlled countries to board a ship, train, or any other transportation as a road to freedom. People trying to escape Hitler's wrath could not get into Britain, not even our land of Palestine (Israel), or Australia, South America or North America. No one wanted us or let us come into their country.

Once the German allied Hungarian regime had control over our area and us, we started being harassed by our neighbors, even though our great-grandparents were raised and lived in the area for centuries amongst these people.

Later, when the Germans disposed of the Hungarian leaders and took control from the Hungarians because they did not trust them, we had no doubt where we stood. Our Jewish hearts broken and bleeding from the constant threats dished out against us, the SS were saying how lazy the Jews were. I don't remember even one lazy Jew in our area, we had to work very hard to sustain ourselves, we were afraid that we were doomed.

Of course there were no jobs available to us at all. Even in our father's tailor shop things were tough. Unfortunately we found out and believed that in Germany in the cities, clubs, fraternal and professional organizations were closed for membership to the Jewish people.

Doors were closed even to people who had not been practicing the Jewish faith even for a generation or more, people whose parents or grandparents had converted and practiced Christianity were treated as enemies. Even those of us who had only Christian friends, people that did not even know that they had even a trace of Jewish blood in them, were singled out and persecuted even more cruelly because they did not want their pure German blood tainted or dirtied. In the city clubs where Jews were already members, any Jew who tried to enter to be with his friends were thrown out. In the city of Munkach suddenly many restaurants refused to serve Jews, because we were considered unclean. The Nazi's preached violence and brutality, resulting in brutal people, rejoining supreme committing the most inhuman and brutal acts.

The same or worst thing happened to us once the German Nazis took over our area. As though the world around us was consumed in hate and viciousness, non-Jewish youths, our former friends, did not want to associate with us or have anything to do with us. Although our families were very close to our Christian neighbors, not only our parents but our grandparents had indeed been friends with them for several generations. Even in our part of Ruthenia, all of a sudden our Christian neighbors and friends became nonchalant, very distant towards us and eventually we were treated by them as strangers or they looked at us as their hated enemies. Things changed for the most part very rapidly everyday something new and more drastic measures were instituted against us.

As usual we met as kids to play, but the atmosphere was not good and all of us Jewish kids were scared and the Christian kids did not want to play with us. You could not help but see and feel the poisonous hat emerging.

It hurt us very deeply, most of all when our neighbors and friends turned their backs on us especially when we needed their understanding, consideration and help. It absolutely crushed us especially me, because my best friend was in the forefront of the Hitler Youth. We could not accept it. Especially those neighbors and friends that had been very close to us and our families had been friends for generations with these people, before this change to fascism. Not too long ago we ate and slept together, played together, worked together, and helped each other when illness or any other needs occurred. No matter what their religious or political views might have been, we were used to being a village of caring friends who cared for each other and looked after each other before the Nazi philosophy onslaught.

We became worried what might be next facing us mainly because during the early Hitler years, there was still time for all of us especially the decent people to oppose the Nazi way of thinking and their criminal actions, but the majority of us and especially the Gentiles were too apathetic and did not become involved. These well meaning, good, decent, God-fearing Christian people just sat back and let others who were not decent do their thinking, acting and even performing the dirty work for them. They were too busy with their own lives to sift through the propaganda about the horror stories we heard and what they did against us Jews, unfortunately these stories had become very real. We had hoped the neighbors would think, or act for themselves, and most of all, stand up for their fellow humans, especially us, their neighbors and friends. In 1943, America and England held a conference in Bermuda to address the Jewish refugee problem, but unfortunately no action was agreed upon. Several organizations pleaded with Churchill and Roosevelt to bomb the railroads leading to the concentration camps, unfortunately, that also went unheeded.

Soon there were all kinds of shortages in our area, especially for us, food which along with clothing became rationed. Jews did not get ration coupons. People had to stand in line for these rationed items and soon they began to grumble, mimic Hitler and put the blame on the Jews for everything.

To me it's still very painful and an unsolved dilemma: how could a people change overnight from good decent humans to vicious monsters? There is no doubt in my mind that apathy by the majority was mostly responsible for Hitler and his fascist cohorts success therefore the ordinary as well as decent people must carry the burden of guilt for the millions of victims of World War II, as well as and especially the Holocaust victims. Decent citizens became fools as well as tools for Fascism, because at first they were delighting in it, and wanted to be part of Hitler's Fascist Germany's success and conquest. Once they became part of it and didn't want to do anything to stop it, maybe they could not change their apathetic ways as a result they became tools and murderers.

The leaders of the free world are not without guilt or blame either. First by playing along with Hitler, first they permitted the annexation of Austria, and then they did not oppose or stop the annexation by Germany of the Sudetenland, and carving up Czechoslovakia. Unfortunately the Allies stood by not stopping Hitler when they could have; then they allowed country after country to fall under the Fascist German onslaught. This was Hitler's hope for the fascist formula to succeed in world domination just what his plan was. The Democratic countries to do nothing and the general population in the free world simply refused to believe that Hitler's ideology could be the way to our and their own possible destruction or demise.

Because of the abuse and attacks upon us, I ran away as a very young boy from the persecution in our village first to our dear Aunt, our Mother's sister, our Uncle and their three lovely children who lived in the town of Vary, near Beregsaz, which was at the original Hungarian border, a few cities removed from us. Unfortunately, my Uncle Weise, Aunt Leichu, along with their three young children perished in the Holocaust. None of them survived. Then when I came home, because I missed my family, they found out and were looking for me, I had to leave again. This time I went to the village of Lavik where we had two uncles and aunts on Father's side along with many cousins. They, along with most of their children also perished at the hand of Hitler. I also stayed with father's sister in that village for a while. She and her husband and ten of their eleven children were murdered in the camps. Again I was very much longing for our family so I went home again thinking that by now it would be okay. But by then things had become intolerable. Again I had to run away this time to Budapest, the capital of Hungary, where I was able to maintain myself somehow without money or relatives living in a large shelter for a while. Then I had to hightail it back home because they were arresting Jewish boys like me because we were not born in Budapest. When I came back home we were constantly and more viciously attacked again and again by the Hitler youth before they took us away.

Of course the world knows now that not only did the Jewish people suffer and die at the hands of the Nazis during World War II, but thousands of non-Jews, including young American soldiers which were killed and crippled. Also, many Germans and their collaborators died from the bombings especially towards the end and on the war fronts. Hundreds of thousands of Jews and Non-Jews from America and other countries were also killed or injured and maimed in the military, fighting against Fascist Germany. Mostly because apathy prevailed and they did not stop Hitler when they could have especially at the start before Fascist dictatorship took over. Once Hitler took absolute control of Germany, he then allied itself with Italy, Japan, Hungary, and other countries, if anyone had dared to oppose the fascists and their criminal acts, it would have also been their end.

Most men, especially the young men in our village, joined the Hitler youth, very enthusiastically, of course the criminals or those on welfare also enthusiastically joined the SS, Gestapo, Einzatz Groupen, or the Werhmacht in order to become one of the German Nazi heroes and be able to perform criminal acts legally. Brutality against us spread like an epidemic. The Fascist became violent and brutal. These brutal men reigned supreme because they had official sanction to permit these horrible acts.

It seemed as though the Germans never considered the possibility that they could also become victims on the battlefields, or from bombings or someday have to bear the responsibility and trials for their criminal actions against fellow humans after the war ended in their defeat and if they did not believe it could happen that Germany eventually could get defeated of course they would all claim they did it for Germany and in the name of Hitler or "Deutschland über Alles" as though it was their duty to follow criminal actions or orders. And no matter which way they looked at it as there is no excuse to became murderers, thieves and criminals. No doubt they did not think they did anything wrong, the same as any thief, rapist or murderer does not think when he performs criminal acts that he could or would be punished for it if caught for the crime.

The facts were and are astounding. When Hitler first ran for national office in Germany he got only 3.5% of the votes. Later, in 1933, even though boisterous Hitler was elected as Chancellor, it was by a very low margin, and Hitler never got a majority of the votes. As a result, political power in Germany passed through default to Hitler and his hateful Fascist followers. Unfortunately, for the human race, and especially for us Jews in Europe, this Nazi power became a lethal weapon not only in the hands of criminals but for most people who became Fascist. Everyone who was a decent person was subject to Nazi abuse in the hands of especially the young criminal rebel-rousers. Yes, Hitler became a dictator and murderer, not by his own hands but at the hands of his loyal followers. He quickly replaced any person who opposed him, or did not do as he dictated, with his own hand-picked henchmen. Once he had control of the German bureaucracy anyone who got in the way of accomplishing his goal was imprisoned, sent into exile or later killed. Anything, and all sorts of crimes, were performed, condoned and permitted in the name of Germany, or Hitler their Fuhrer. Für Deutschland. "For the Fatherland." For Germany.

Now back to the things that caught us in a trap. In our village of Palanok, this was changed to Va'r Pola'nko when Fascist Hungary took over. As soon as they arrived many changes took place. When our area was part of Czechoslovakia, the building adjoining our backyard first housed and was a meeting hall for the union members or labor party, then it housed the communist party and now it became the head quarters and training center of the Hitler youth and the Nazi Party, which made it more difficult for us having these hate mongers next door.

When Hitler started to take over other countries or territories in Europe like our area, these devoted Communist Party members in our village, who were of decent German origin, most of them instantly became Fascist. They enthusiastically embraced and became part of Hitler's Nazi ruling party. Obviously their children became the stronghold for the Hitler Youth and now we know this was the main reason the Germans were so confident they could defeat everyone to take over control not only of our area but most of Europe and indeed they almost succeeded to be the eventual rulers of Europe and then the world.

Our area was taken over, occupied by Hungary because they became one of the Nazi German allies along with Italy, Japan, etc. As a result, the local Schwaben indirectly, but immediately became Nazis who then took control. Suddenly our village became a different place in which to live or really just exist. Part of the Hungarians Fascist leader, Saloshi's, edict was preparing themselves militarily for conquering adjoining areas from Rumania, Poland, Ukrainian, etc. The Hungarian, or Zondarmed militia, suddenly became sadistic and they used brute force against us Jews and they made all of us boys report once a week for Levente paramilitary training at the age of eleven. However, there was one exception; in our village the Christian (mostly Schwaben) youth were given wooden guns first and taught to use it, to march proudly, wear the swastikas, how to salute their Nazi superiors with our outstretched raised arms shouting "Heil Hitler," and how to become good, loyal Nazi soldiers.

We, the Jewish boys on the other hand, at the age of eleven and up had to report for abusive work training. We were given shovels and forced to dig ditches, to clean latrines, and to do other menial or dirt clean-up jobs that were degrading to ordinary citizens, especially to the Germans. Most of the German boys were encouraged by their parents to join the Hitler "Yugent" Youth Movement. They were convinced that they could go up the ladder faster and eventually become leaders of the Third Reich and be part of the rulers of the world for a thousand years if they joined Hitler's elite early in their lives. Obviously that is what most of them did and did it very enthusiastically. They referred proudly to this era as their "Thousand Year Third Reich." Pictures surfaced later of Jews being beheaded, hanged, tortured, or maimed, with obscene inscriptions written on them.

We had very close German friends and neighbors for many years indeed for several generations not only in our village but also in the adjoining town of Munkach and especially the other close by villages and towns. But suddenly, when the Nazis took over, the Christian friends did not visit us regularly, most surprisingly not even to get their clothes made, fixed or even altered in my Father's best very popular tailor shop. Most of all even those that did not join the Fascist organization or were not German did nothing to stop Fascism, they did not protest, resist or speak out against the anti Jewish acts against us that were happening in front of their eyes, shockingly some were enthusiastic participants, but with most, apathy prevailed everywhere even amongst the God-fearing, good, religious Christian people.

The Hungarians started drafting people of military age for Munka Tabor labor camp, but that was only a prelude as to what's in store for us. First our Father was drafted and then our oldest three brothers Fishi, Ben, and Bernie, also were drafted and taken away to the Hungarian labor camps because they were Jews of military age. Later for some reason they let our father come home.

In late 1943 or early 1944 the Nazis were not satisfied with the way the Hungarians were collaborating in their war effort against Russia or the way in which they were handling or disposing of the Jews. Suddenly, without any warning, they replaced the Hungarian leaders, military officers, some soldiers and the non-coms overnight in our area. Then the bad got worse. We lived directly under the SS Gestapo and Einzats Groupen complete rule which was even more repressive and unbearable than before. This tore our Mother up. First she worried silently, then she used to go into the barn to get away from us as she was crying hysterically but she did not want to upset us, or to let us see her crying.

As Hitler's youth groups became more assertive, boisterous and more popular, the Hitler youth in our village began to vent more of their power and hatred on everyone that was not of pure German heritage. Most of their hatred was, of course, first targeted especially toward the Jewish youth, exposing us to very traumatic experiences by attacking us in gangs. These were the same people who had once been our very close friends and neighbors. The Fascist youth traveled in groups, especially when they came out of their meetings and propaganda training at the Hitler Youth hall, the school, or church. Anytime they saw us Jews anywhere or would pass us on the street, they would attack us in force and try to outdo each other in their raceist, hateful, Fascist ways. They would throw stones hit us or attack us in gangs. Especially against the younger, my age, Jewish children and the elderly who were also common targets, because there were only a few of us and so many of them most of the time we were not able to stand up to such large Fascist groups when attached. After all we were a very small minority in our village.

Even during this depressive time many times we had beggars pass our village to beg for food or money. Even they had to stop coming because of the attacks. We still worked very hard six days a week then Friday we would clean up and prepare for the Holy Sabbath with extra food whenever possible for the travelers, strangers, or people passing our village especially those Jews that escaped the problems and executions in adjoining Poland or other countries close by us.

It was amazing and it stunned us, we could not get over it, to see how proud our neighbors, former friends, the parents of these Nazi youth became. In good weather they would sit or stand outside and watch their children or friends as they threw rocks, mud and other items at the passing Jewish people or as they attacked our homes. It was especially hurtful because they and their children were formerly our friends, and now they became bullies, Jew-haters, and were encouraged by their parents by their silence in acts against us even though we were their neighbors and friends for generations just because we were of a different faith, nationalities or backgrounds.

Hatred was not only being taught at the Hitler Youth Club Meetings but no doubt also had to be espoused in their homes and their village community meetings. It seemed that throughout our entire village the Swabish people became bigots, anti-Semites, and haters of their fellow man. Even neighbors that were not of German decent became anti-Semitic. There seemed to be no end to the hate epidemic. They strive to disturb our Holy Sabbath which especially upset our mother terribly because when she was getting ready to light the Sabbath candles to remind us to remember and observe the Holy day they were outside shouting obscenities, throwing rocks in our home.

If the Fascists in our area wanted to get rid of a neighbor, whether Jewish, Ruthenian, Gypsy, or any other nationality, he could simply turn him in to the Gestapo. He would tell them that the accused was a communist, a Jew, or if not that then a Jew-lover, or anyone that was undesirable to them. This person would be arrested and often never be heard from again.

We, the Jewish people, were not even allowed to purchase newspapers and were barred from every form of communication. We were not even allowed to own a radio, and those things were confiscated from us. Of course we had never even heard of television at that time, and in fact, radios were a rarity in our village, now that everything had become censored and forbidden to us. There were very few telephones in our village, most of them were at the Post Office and only the Fascists, government employees, or people in the military bases were allowed to have telephones and radios or use them. Our only way of communicating with anyone was by "word of mouth" and unfortunately the only news we got day in and day out was bad for us. We still hoped that soon this hatred would disappear and Christian principals of truth and common humanity would prevail.

Since so many dialects and languages were spoken in our region sometimes, one group could hardly understand the other. It was difficult to believe the terrible rumors that were circulating in our area. We were hearing about Jews being killed or massacred by the thousands. In the town's villages and camps in Poland, Germany, Romania, Ukrainian, Kazakhstan, Galitzia, Lithuania, etc., we were told that our people there were being wiped out. These rumors were spreading like wild fire but we could not believe it and unfortunately, we know now, they were true.

Our beloved Mother and Father became more fearful and worried for us, their children, with each passing day. Each time we (any of us brothers) were attacked or accosted on the street by the Hitler Youth's (which occurred many times of course by our former friends), they worried more and more for us, sometimes they were petrified if we did not show up on time from school, synagogue, or other places. Rumors of arrests, deportation, rape, pillage, confiscation and murder were not so much a rumor any more only in other countries. We began to see and experience that type of treatment and happenings more often. Just like any other young boys and girls, we were curious and went snooping outside but, all of us really began to fear for our lives, even going to the Synagogue was an ordeal, going to see your neighbor, we could not even take our cow to pasture or just trying to locate some food was a scary ordeal.

Before they were drafted into the Labor camps, my older brothers and our employees from my father's tailor shop were the most daring Jewish boys in our village. They tried to fight back, no matter how much they were outnumbered, certainly Jews were not permitted guns even with bare hands they would stand their ground against many of the Fascist attackers which of course made matters that much worse for us. Father would warn us and urge us not to overreact to the attacks whether they outnumbers us or not because they had the Hungarian Fascist authorities, the "Zondarmed," and the German soldiers on their side who had guns ready and anxious to shoot us. Even we, the younger ones, were urged and warned not to fight back; in other words just keep out of their way.

Father taught us if the Hitler Youth or military men lifted up their hands to attack us, we should lift up our legs to run away as fast as we could. And in our misery our parents not only worried about us, they also worried for their relatives whom we had not heard from in the haven called the U.S.A. We did not know what was going on with them because it was forbidden to be in touch with Americans or anyone anywhere. The Fascist publicity was saying that people in America were starving, they were without jobs, and many were losing their homes and committing suicide fighting amongst themselves and most of all that the Americans did not care what happened to us.

By this time the Jewish adults felt certain the people of the free world ignored or just did not care what happens to us because we were told, that the leaders in the free democratic countries, such as America, England, France, etc. had been informed and had full knowledge and evidence of our plight about the killing centers against the Jews in Poland, Ukraine, Germany, etc. They must have known about Hitler's plan to eradicate all the Jews and other minorities in all of Europe. We heard more and more about these killing centers located mostly in eastern Europe, especially in Poland and Lithuania, close to us where most of the world's Jewish population them lived. Extermination centers like, Sobior, Mardanck, Beletz, Treblinka, as well as names of forests were popping up everywhere. The allies no doubt could have, and should have, stopped Hitler from killing our people before it became too late for over eleven million American people that were either killed, maimed or injured or suffered during W.W.II. What makes this even more shocking and tragic is that these inhumanities were carried out with such vengeance, openly and without shame by the German Nazi's. If the Allies had wanted to especially initially it would have been easy to have stopped it when the Nazi's started and boasted about the pogrom of open suppression.

Didn't people especially in America, care to know what was going on? Or didn't they care what was happening to us and millions of other innocent people, including their relatives? We were sure that the entire world knew. We only hoped they would act quickly to stop the slaughter of our people and us before it was too late to defeat the German's. They should not have allowed blood on their hands, even if it was the blood of Jews.

Even as a kid I remember hearing that almost every Jewish family in Germany or their collaborators in occupied in Europe were trying to get papers to exit Europe, to leave and be free of the haters and killers. Mostly they tried to get into Palestine which was bequeathed to us by the Almighty through Moses this was then under British control it was the desire of most Jews to go there. After all Palestine (Israel) was our Jewish homeland for thousands of years, home of our forefathers; Abraham, Jacob, and Moses. But unfortunately it was not open to us to immigrate there. Tragically the British occupiers did not allow entry because they collaborated with the Arabs.

If Jews were not permitted entry to their own homeland of Palestine, then where could we expect to go? The Germans had us trapped, perhaps unknowingly, but we got caught in the trap that would assure them that we would cooperate with them. The Jews tried to immigrate and to escape to any other country, especially to Israel, England, America, Canada, South America, Australia, New Zealand, South Africa, any country that would allow entry, but we were not allowed into any country. Most of the Jewish people we knew tried to leave fascist Europe and to get away from Hitler's hate mongers and killers. Every Jew's dream was to get out of Eastern Europe as quickly as possible, yet it seemed that no country wanted us. All ports were closed to us. Even America, Cuba, other Latin Countries, Canada and Great Britain closed their doors to us the pleading desperate Jews. Even those that were of military age signed up and wanted to fight with the Allied Armies tried to flee from Germany and its occupied fascists territories but we were not allowed entry, not even the partisans wanted us. In fact my three oldest brothers, as well as millions of others of military age would have been happy to join the allied military to fight against Nazi Germany. No country anywhere wanted to help or accept us Jews even though a lot of them knew it was for us certain death if we stayed in German occupied or its allied countries.

Being such a young boy I was wondering was it because we were Jewish did the Allies hate us too, or was it because we were known as the chosen people as I was taught in Hebrew School. Surely our friends and neighbors were not afraid of Hitler's wrath? We were caught in the trap, and we could not imagine decent people throughout the world not caring about the plight of so many of us humans, especially those of us young innocent children, the women or the elderly, after all we could not have hurt anyone. Surely our family in America cared about us. Also the girl, Janet, I met when she visited our village and I fell in love with her. She lives in America. Surely she cared.

At the beginning, before World War II broke out, very few of the very rich or lucky ones left somehow and found passage to Cuba, America, or the English shores. We heard that at first they were reaching those hallowed shores safely, and were permitted entry, but later we found out that the ships bringing immigrants to freedom were forced to return from Cuba and America back to Europe with their human cargo and no doubt probably to their death. We also heard that some of the ships filled with people fleeing Nazi Germany were torpedoed, by the German's, at sea and all the people on board were killed. We heard about the Wannsee conference, when Hitler tested the world by offering to give up the Jews for a fee. Hardly any nation took him up on his offer. This was again proof to Hitler that no country wanted Jews.

One documented event we found out after the war ended was of the ship "St. Louis," whose destination was first Cuba where the passengers even with valid visas to enter Cuba were denied entry. Then the ship stopped on American shores for two weeks pleading with American authorities to be permitted to disembark, many of them had relatives here, and stay till the war was over. But no entry was permitted for those Jews. The ship finally returned to Europe with 937 Jewish men, women, and many young children on board. Upon their return to Germany, they were met at the dock and most were taken immediately to the concentration camps in order to "teach the Jews and the world a lesson." Most of them perished in the Holocaust but unfortunately the free world did not care to do anything to save us. There were hundreds of thousands of unfilled immigration quotas for America in countries under Hitler's rule.

Very few Jewish people were able to exit Europe at that time and just a very few of the ones who escaped managed to reach safe haven in the Jewish homeland known then as Palestine, or anywhere else. How could Jews escape Hitler's Reich if there was no place for us to go?

This was for sure the turning event. Hitler proved his point; he was boasting that no country, including America, wanted to let us Jews in, which gave him and his Fascist cohorts the encouragement and green light to proceed with the world's peoples' blessing to liquidate the Jews, and then other nationalities in all of Europe.

Our oldest brother, Philip, could have and probably would have had a visa and leave for America early in the war years, but he decided to stay with our family and to help father out in his tailor shop because he had so many mouths to feed so he stayed no matter what dangers he faced. That must have been life's hardest decision for him to give up the opportunity to leave for the golden land of America. Maybe he could have lived safely in America, even if it was without the family. Nevertheless, he decided to stay with us in spite of the terrible rumors, hopefully to survive and be liberated with us as a family by the Allies, we all thought and hoped that Fascist Germany would be defeated real soon but unfortunately it dragged on and only got worse.

Our Uncle Yosef, and his family, who also lived in our village and was very close with us, started in secret to slaughter cattle the kosher way and to provide kosher meat for us and Jews in our adjoining town and villages which was absolutely prohibited by the Nazis. He was joined by our brother Ben.

I also helped many times as a very young boy to deliver the kosher meat with a bicycle to people in the city before dawn. Many times I took our sister Rosalyn very early in the morning to the city's Hebrew Academy on the bike at the same time. It was very difficult for me. We had to leave early dawn especially in the winter because of the snows and cold weather to peddle a bike to deliver meat and to take Rosalyn to school was very taxing on me.

Our family along with a few others were an exception because we were gutsy and stood up against the barbaric Nazi Youth and because of that I first had to run away and leave our village in the early afternoon walking many miles and hooking up with a farmer, his buggy and cows, not arriving till next morning at my Uncle's place. On the way we were stopped by a pack of wolves that scared the hell out of us. Luckily they had matches which we lit at the same time to disburse and scare them before we could go on and stay for a while with our two Aunts and Uncles. One of them had nine or ten children, the other had four. I had lots of cousins in Lavik. I longed for my family so I went back home as soon as I could.

When they discovered that I was home I had to leave again. I went to our Aunt and Uncle and their children and their children many miles away from us in Vary, which was near a town called Beregsaz. Of course I was really longing for my Mother, Dad, brothers and sister. When I came back the attacks on us became more vicious and more frequent.

Looking back I feel that our older brothers would at least have left for America, or would have tried to escape had they believed the horrible rumors of the hell awaiting us. We were convinced that the occupier of our territory, the "Saloshi" Hungarian Nazi Regime, would not turn us over to the German

Gestapo. We thought the Hungarians, while anti-Semitic enough, were our neutral allies. After all, we were hard working, decent people, good neighbors, good citizens of Hungary, and we were liked by most of the people in our Schwaben villages. We got along with everyone and most of all we thought they would be treating Jews fairly. There were over 700,000 Jews in Hungary in 1943.

I felt our only crime in life, then it seems was one in which we had no control over. We were born to Jewish parents and were of Jewish faith. We did not believe that when all of the new political changes were made we would end up being punished for being Jewish. Little did we know that our neighbors, especially the Schwaben neighbors, would become such fervent Fascists and suddenly hate us for no good reason except that we were Jews and they were convinced that they, along with Hitler, would take complete control and become leaders of the world.

This venom was spouting out from them and happened soon after they became Nazis after joining Hitler's party because they were given the upper hand over us by the SS, suddenly in 1943 the Germans did not trust even their own allies or families, so they took over and deposed of the Hungarian Horty regime and took over all military and civilian rules, even from the Fascist Hungarians, everything concerning the Jews, especially in our area.

We expected and hoped to be liberated any moment. Rumors were rampant that the Russian army was very close. In our imagination we heard heavy guns go off and we saw night and day the German military with heavy equipment going towards the Russian front and we were counting days and nights, hoping that we would be liberated any day.

We were tortured psychologically by the Hungarians, Hitler youth and SS Einzats Groupen, as well as The Hungarian Zondarmed, and German soldiers, especially those stationed in the bastion and military base close to us. When they were drunk they came to our home and other Jewish homes demanding money, gold and other valuables.

Now that the German Army had control of our area soon thereafter one early morning there was a knock on our door. Some military men came with a local Nazi who had designs on our father's tailor shop. They wanted to take out Father away, but my sister, Rosalyn cried and hung onto his leg and refused to let them take him away. She was carrying and screaming. By that time, our older brothers arrived with a few of Father's other employees, and the "gendarme" Hungarian militia left with that man, fortunately without our father.

By this time the Hungarian soldiers wanted to be mean just like the Germans, they came from the Military base in the adjoining city and the bastion overlooking our village to harass us. We had, of course, been turned in as Jewish people. The military age Jews were by then drafted for the Hungarian labor camp "Munko Tabor." They sent father notice to report for military labor. Soldiers came first for father. They told him that he was to leave for the Labor Camps immediately. One of the soldiers who were sent for him had been a patron of Father's. He had tailored his army suits for him which made it for that soldier painful to take him away, but he did it anyway. Father was the first of our family to be drafted and taken to the labor camps. I remember the day that Father left. We were all scared, crying and praying for his safety and return. There was much concern for his safety, yet he left with dignity. We all cried and begged him not to go. We also begged the soldier not to take him away from us but he took him anyway.

It was several weeks before we heard from him because communication amongst forbidden. Finally after a few months they let him return home to us, a weak sick and pale man. The hard physical work under the Hungarian fascist military at the Russian front had taken its toll on him.

One by one other male members of our family were drafted and taken to the work camps. Our oldest brother Philip was next drafted to go to the labor camp, then Ben who was living away from home but he returned from Budapest.

I also ran away to the capitol of Hungary, where I saw him only a few times. He was also taken. Next brother Bernie who was sort of weak was also drafted and taken away because he was over eighteen, to the labor camps of course this broke our mothers, and our hearts. Again it was very rare that we heard from them.

We were politically naive and not worldly. Our parents were convinced that the wonderful pious, very religious Rabbi's would perform miracles and save us. After all, the revered chief rabbi of Munkach, who was against Zionism, was speaking out against people wanting to go to Israel back when they could. He felt that the Messiah would soon deliver us from our oppressors to our promised land.

Fortunately our father was permitted to stay home after a few months. Father did not speak of the Labor camps when he came back. We did not know for a long time what had happened to him because he did not want us to worry about the fate of our three brothers. But as each of my three older brothers were taken away to the labor camps, he opened up and gave a scratchy account of what had happened to him in the labor camp run by Hungarian Jew haters.

He told us of the very hard work the Hungarian military subjected them to from early sun up to late sun down, of beatings, and abuse, and very little food, of dogs that were especially trained to attacked and bite if you tried to deviate from the work area or escape. These dogs were trained for attacks if you strayed only a few feet away from work or camp area assigned to them. The Hungarian Guards, arrow crossed bandits, would shoot to kill for the slightest infraction or misdeed by a Jew. They behaved just like the Nazi bandits.

It was always a happy day when a loved one returned from the labor camps, especially from the cold winter from the icy wasteland of Russia. We were especially delighted when our Father returned. He was able to relate to us, but reluctantly, first hand the facts about what he and other Jews had to endure under the Hungarian Fascist. Little did we realize that he was considered old at 45, they sent him home I guess later to be taken away with us to the extermination camps.

Food was in very short supply all over Europe and our area was no exception. Most able bodies people eighteen or older, were taken for the military or labor camps, there were very few young able bodied people to work the farm fields, the factories or mines and food ration coupons became a dire necessity for the citizens of our area. However, Jewish people were not given ration coupons, thus forcing father to buy food on the black market; which meant he paid several times more than what the normal price was or should be; mostly luckily, he was bartering food for tailoring work. We did not have much money so it was fortunate when he was able to buy a few potatoes, a little flour for Mother to make bread, or other basic staples by bartering tailor work, or other valuables for them. A few shriveled carrots, beans, cabbage, and miracle of miracles, sometimes a kosher chicken for Sabbath. It was a delight when soup or stew became available. To acquire just basic food was wonderful in itself, if we were able to procure it. Just to be able to keep us alive with basic necessities was a difficult chore. We were lucky because some former friends and especially Ruskie speaking farming people from the surrounding village liked us and especially my father's tailoring. Somehow we managed to secure enough food to keep us going.

There were occasionally times I had some fun even in these turbulent times. I took our milk cow out to pasture to a field where someone's maid, in her thirties or older, had also taken their cows. She started to play with me and I was flabbergasted and confused when she aroused me sexually. I was about twelve years old; however she made me feel heavenly even though it was only for a few minutes before I had to get back to the realities and the miseries of Fascism confronting us.

Towards the end of 1943 there was no way for us to make a decent living because if anyone was caught dealing with a persona non grata merchant (a Jew) he would be frowned on by neighbors and certain to be boycotted by the Fascist Intelligence and I had to leave our home a few times. Each day became harder than the previous one for all of us Jews in our village. Even if this is where we had been born and our family lived here many generations. Even our great-grandparents were born and always lived here in this home.

All of us tried very hard to keep the Sabbath Holy we were brought up that it's the most important day of the week. Father smoked a pipe six days a week but Friday father cleaned all his pipes, filled them with fresh tobacco put them away, and did not touch them until the Sabbath had passed. When the Havadalah candles were lit to signify Sabbath was over, he picked up his pipe and lit it again. Our problems intensified under the Fascist regime.

Sometimes our employees and brothers had to go into the fields at night to search for food such as potatoes, corn, string beans, beets; that might have been left by the farmers. After all we were a large family had to have food to keep us alive. Unfortunately, none of the allies wanted to extend a helping hand even though we heard that Eichmann and the Germans wanted to trade the Jews for Money.

We heard stories that the Germans bombed a church in Poland by accident, and when the clergymen found out about it, the Christians cried for revenge against the perpetrators. But when the Germans, damaged and destroyed our Jewish synagogues, our homes and were brutalizing us as early as 1933 on Kristal Nacht. Our Christian neighbors hardly noticed or certainly ignored it and they uttered not one word of protest, if anything they took delight in it. Certainly they did nothing about it. Then the Nazis youth even destroyed Jewish cemeteries for kicks. They would not even leave our dead in peace, you could not help but notice the Nazi sympathizers as well as the ordinary citizens were overjoyed or participated enthusiastically in them and with those Hitler Youth.

Only a while ago the German army was boisterous no matter how the war went they were growing mentally and militarily stronger with each country that they invaded and conquered. Town after town, village after village, was being taken over by the cocky elite German soldiers. With each victory the Nazi Party member and especially the military grew stronger and wealthier taking or confiscating from the conquered people, especially the Jews, many of their valuables and shipping most of it to Germany.

The Nazis not only gained for the most part the unconditional support of their own people at home but also most of the people they conquered were subjugated who became Nazi sympathizers. The Germans in 1942-43 looked invincible, and thus the soldiers were encouraged to keep on fighting and conquering.

With each military they also enriched themselves by confiscating at first money from the Jews then from other and keeping for themselves priceless art, jewelry, antiques, buildings, furniture, and land. All these things, they supposedly did in the name of Hitler the Fuhrer, and "For Germany." Everything was taken, first from the Jewish people, then from uncooperative Gentiles who did not agree with Hitler or Fascism. Those with opposing political opinions also had their possessions taken away and were sent away to prison or work camp.

Everything that decent people consider illegal was made legal by the Nazi's to further their cause of "Deutschland über Alles"--Germany over Everything. We learned later that most banks in the occupied areas were closed by the conquering armies, and the monies, stocks, especially from the Jews, and valuables were passed into the hand of Germany's Hitler and their collaborators.

There is no doubt that most of our Jewish people's art work, gold and other valuables became for the most part their personal possessions. Especially cash, diamonds, rubies, and other precious stones that were confiscated before or after they killed our Jewish people much of it was given by the conquerors to their wives or girlfriends especially the SS soldiers in charge of us or shipped it to Germany a lot of it was even found hidden in the camps that they did not have time to distribute, to send home or overseas such as Latin America or Switzerland.

There is also no doubt in my mind that what booties and cash they took away from us Jews and others in the occupied countries financed most of the war of attrition against humanity as well as it has left Germany, for Switzerland, financed their industry and its people prosperous then and even to this day. History has proven that the German ground soldiers were the best trained for war and attrition in the world at that time because they had devoted a great deal time and resources to it. Huge ships, like the "Bismarck," patrolled the shores of Germany, and Hitler and his military people felt very confident in doing just what he wanted to do. First to conquer Europe, and then to conquer the remainder of the world.

The world has found out that their plan, first and foremost, was to gather all of the Jewish people to be killed and rid Europe of them. Then they would decide who they would want to be next disposed of. Maybe the gypsies or the Latins, nearby Slavs, and then who would be next? After eliminating the Jews they felt confident that they could pick any religion, race, nationality of anyone who did not fit into the pure Aryan German race category or Nazi ideology.

All of us Jews were still trying to run away to hide, escape or run for dear life from our oppressors but there was no place to run or hide. Unfortunately we knew no one wanted us; there was no place for us on the face of this earth. No matter how many times I ran away, or where I went they caught up with me even in the Hungarian capitol of Budapest. First they started to round up Jews who were not from there. I had to return home before I got caught in the trap. When I arrived home it was March 1944, just before Passover when we celebrate and commemorate the Exodus from Egypt using special dishes silverware and utensils. Everything has to be especially prepared. We were very scared as to what is in store for us. Just as the last day of Passover arrived we did not even have a chance to put up in the attic the Passover dishes and utensils away, when they came and rounded up all Jews from our village and areas, then we were taken first to the ghetto which was a short stop on the road to the worst hell in the history on this earth.

Just before we were arrested and taken to the ghetto we learned through rumors that our brothers Ben, Philip and Bernie are OK and they were still in the Hungarian labor camps but probably under more strict German control somewhere along the Russian front digging ditches on the fighting front line and performing other dangerous slave labor.

In spite of our plight, now in the ghetto, Father and Mother were worried about them just as they, our brothers, must have worried about us. We could not even get information about them when we were at home because any information coming to us was censored or twisted.

Word of mouth information came to us only when people were discharged or let out because of sickness from the labor camps, some escaped or arrived home for leave. Sometimes information we got was months old, but at least we heard once in a while, when we were still in our home that they were alive which was most heartwarming to us and especially to our Mom and Dad who were terribly worried about their children.

As we were taken from our home, it was very painful to bid goodbye to our home, our land, and our precious possessions, our neighbors; even though most of them became Fascist. Our heart was shattered when we were made to march under Hungarian and German guards towards what we found out later as a ghetto a temporary abode on the road to demise.

Our life from then on changed completely and inhumanely. We were put through hell on earth that is beyond belief even by today's world horrors. Those that survived the hell on earth describe the suffering we endured.

The village, city, and people I loved when I got my start and learned to cherish my Jewish or Yiddish life, is now abandoned and expelling us. They want to make us *"Judenrein"* (free of Jews). The world and life we were born to was shattered and lost. But they cannot take my memories away from me, which hopefully will help me on the road to a good maturity. Yes, we were backwards and naive, then yes, unfortunately, the Nazi's imagination goes us.

They became killers, we became the victims. At first they forced us to wear yellow stars; they took us for exploitation to the ghettos. What was worse was the train ride and the cattle cares, and even worse the total dehumanization in Auschwitz.

The camp sufferings were the worst and we endured more than anyone in the annals of history. Then of course, the gas chambers, and death marches, and I cannot describe to normal people what I saw and experienced. No one would believe me to know that people could do these horrible things to another person.

Chapter 3: Ghetto

I shall never forget the early spring bitter cold dreary day and how the elders, especially our calm wise parents were suddenly petrified when "they" came for the naive Jews, to arrest us and take us away from our home, which we did not believe would happen, to take us to what later we discovered was a new make shift ghetto, just at the end of out eight day Passover Holiday. It was probably the most dismal Passover and scary day we had ever known until then. Our father could not believe how quickly and completely the German people changed after all he worked with them in Vienna Austria, where he learned his tailoring trade and our village was mostly German, so we were brought up with Germans and got along with them.

Four years prior to our arrest and deportation to the ghetto we saw many changes in our village, how people, even our decent neighbors changed from caring good people to uncaring, vicious fascist creatures, we experienced in those last few years very scary things that were happening to us, but nothing like being forced from our home by guards pointing loaded guns and bayonets at us, making us line up to be accounted for then taking us first to a temporary place without shelter or roof over our head, and nothing to keep us warm during this chilly weather. The Hungarian Horty government, which was fully cooperating with Hitler's Germany Axis when they annexed took away and occupied our area from Czechoslovakia, were replaced suddenly in 1943 by another Hungarian Fascist dictatorial government, headed by its boisterous leader, Saloshi. Ever since Hungary took control of our part of Europe on March 19, 1941 from Czechoslovakia (when it was carved up), the Hungarians held and ruled under Nazi German control our area until late 1943, and as the Russians became victorious, The Hungarian leaders Horty made a pact with Russia.

Hitler, in late 1943, suddenly stopped trusting his allies which included the fascist Hungarians, even though the fascist Saloshi regime had taken control from Premier Horty, the previous Regent and Hungarian leader. The Saloshi regime were true fascists, cooperating completely in the war effort against Russia, and were solidly on Nazi Germany's side to take over and rule all of Europe especially in instigating their anti-Jewish actions and edicts. The Nazis would not allow the Jews to be liberated and unfortunately the Red Army took its time to save us.

Even prior to the German Army taking over complete control, the strict Hungarian Fascists enforced harsh anti-Semitic edicts against us Jews, and it became worse when the Saloshi Nazi government took over from the somewhat democratic Hungarian Regent Horty when he was, in effect, deposed. When the German SS took over complete control from the Hungarian Army around January of 1944, we were promised by the Germans if we behave and cooperate, we would have better living conditions, better housing, and most of all sufficient food which was rationed, (even to the Christians) but we Jews did not get ration coupons, so as a result we were not able to buy even the bare staples to provide sufficient food for our families' sustenance, not to mention being able to sustain decent living quarters, as we had even lost our maid. We were not even allowed to hire help. Our mother had to cook, clean, wash by hand everything for a dozen or more people. We did not have running water or own things like washers, dryers, dishwashers or any of the luxuries available today.

The SS told us before we were rounded up, that we would be relocated away from our Jew-hating anti-Semitic neighbors, who became openly and ferociously anti-Semitic, especially those Schwaben of German decent. The SS promised that after we were relocated we could live tranquilly in our new and better housing in a peaceful atmosphere, and that they would provide a good place for us to work, decent housing, and work no doubt utilizing our skills. Yes, it seemed "too good to be true." But what choice did we really have? We could go nowhere. Certainly not to Poland, which was only twenty or thirty miles away; it was rumored to be a sure graveyard for all Jews. We could not trust the Ruskies to turn us in, or the Hungarian Fascists. We also heard rumors that there were no more Jews left in any of the countries adjoining us such as Czechoslovakia, Austria, Yugoslavia, Poland, Galitzia, even Romania, and especially in neighboring Lithuania, Ukraine or in German occupied Russia. Posters appeared in the center of our village that all Jews are to be ready for shipment to Germany but first to be located to the ghetto.

The big question in our minds before they took us away from our homes and brought us to the miserable ghetto was whether a Jew would be welcome now anywhere in this world. After all, our own German Schwabish neighbors and former friends became hate mongers, especially against us Jews. They were happy in our sorrow, and it was even more painful when we saw them smirk and root on the SS and Hungarian guards as we were forced from our homes, loosing everything our parents and grandparents saved for.

It was a constant concern for us but especially to our parents about our older three brothers Philip, Ben and Bernie. Mother and Father were mumbling to each other asking questions. Where and how were our other young and able bodied 18 to 45 year old Jewish male relatives, especially their three oldest sons, our three brothers, who were drafted the year before and taken away from us to the Hungarian labor camps? We constantly worried and wondered what was happening to them and where they were, whether they were alive or in what condition they were in. Would they be spared or protected by the Hungarians, especially under the new circumstances, or were they also doomed for extinction? We were under house arrest, so of course the biggest worry we had now was what they were going to do with us or to us, when and how, or where were they going to take us from here which was formerly our home and place of birth?

Was there any truth to what the SS said to us and promised us? That we will be taken to a decent place to work and live that we will be provided sufficient food and shelter? Or were the horrible rumors we heard really true? We heard of mass killing centers of Jews in Poland, Russia, Lithuania, Ukraine etc. We heard of Jews dying of starvation in the ghettos. We also of the shooting in the forests and the killing centers called concentration camps to which we might be taken. We had no idea where we might be taken, but we were scared out of our wits, over what was next in store for us.

We were horrified before and as we were brought here, to see our Christian neighbors' kids and former friends happily watching us behind the ghetto fences. There wasn't even a trace of pity in their faces. No shock. Not one Christian protested, voiced opposition or showed anger over what was happening to us, or certainly we did not see it, nor were they interested in helping us. There is no doubt some of our long time friends and neighbors could have helped us by throwing us bread or some potatoes to help us through our plight, but to our dismay, most of them were smirking. How could they be so indifferent to their neighbors? To our suffering and possible extinction?

In spite of the terrible predicament we found ourselves in, we were quite focused and our mother and father especially were worried about our three older brothers who were taken away to the Hungarian labor camps, just as they, our brothers, must have been worried about us. We could not get information about them, nor could they get information about us, because any and all information coming to us or leaving was censored. Before we were taken to the ghetto, information via word of mouth sometimes came to us when people were discharged from the labor camps; some were let out because of sickness, escaped or arrived home for leave. Sometimes information we got was months old but at least we heard once in awhile when we were still in our home that our brothers were alive and ok, which was most heartwarming to us, but especially to our Mom and Dad who were "sick with worry" about their children.

Naturally, the horrible rumors sounded more realistic now that we were imprisoned in a brick factory that they converted to the ghetto. We were scared out of our wits, because of the abusive treatment we got here the SS were screaming "Far Shtunkene, Yuden," ("stinking Jews") and we became very frightened as to what was in store for us! We still hoped that all these terrible rumors about all the Jews being killed and tortured in the concentration camps in Poland and other areas was not true!

Now in the ghetto, we remembered that only a few days after totally taking over from the Hungarians, the local Fascist in our area took great pride and joy from the new German Government, especially from its special "Einzatz Groupen" Jew killing units. They along with the local Nazi collaborators and the SS, with the full cooperation of the Hungarian Zondarmed, reaffirmed to us that we were taken first to a ghetto as a temporary place to stay. They again told us that after a short while here in the ghetto we would be moved to a permanent place to "Deutschland the Fatherland" Germany, where we would be accepted and treated decently just as other humans and that they would take care of all of our necessities especially work, housing, food, etc. They said that Jewish people would be treated equally, as well as any of the other citizens; and that they tool us away to protect us from the local right-wing Jew-haters additionally we were assured that we would be able to use our work skills to better ourselves because they needed good tradesmen such as good tailors, construction and other trades people which we were.

Above all, they told us they needed good workers, because most of their German loyal people were in the military hoping to take over Europe first and then move on to conquer the world. They wanted us to believe that the ghetto would be a temporary gathering place for our Jewish people, and that living conditions would be much better for us when we arrived at our new and permanent homes. We were also told that wholesome food, decent homes and good jobs would be available. They made it sound almost believable. They promised us much better conditions than what we had been exposed to in the ghetto. This would have been welcomed by us, as we had to endure terrible consequences under the Fascist Hungarian regime especially from the local Schwaben Hitler youth. I shall never forget that I had to run away several times from our home and village from the hateful hands of the local Hitler youth, our former friends and neighbors who had become fervent fascists and Jew-haters. The last few years we were exposed to and endured the constant Hitler Youth bating; fascist harassment's and we were subjected to many attacks, abuse, name calling and shortages of all kinds, especially food and what was the worst, the completely changed friendly neighbors to hate mongers.

Before they took us to the ghetto, a special German army unit arrived and took over our area. At first we were told by these German special "Einzatz Groupen" soldiers, (not knowing they were Special Jew Killing Units) that when and if we were to be relocated, we should take all of our money, jewelry, important valuables and possessions with us. But the Hungarian Fascists, especially the Saloshi soldiers and local Nazi leaders, as well as our former friends and neighbors, told us to take only the minimum: a change of clothing, a small amount of food for a day or so, and a few essential items with us. They would keep everything safe for us till we get back or they would send it to us if we want it, no wonder we were so dumbfounded and confused.

We were told several times by our neighbors to leave everything except the very essentials at home and soon, after the war is over, we could come back for it and reclaim it. Furthermore they assured us that during the time we were away our possessions would be guarded and overseen very carefully by them. If we like the place we will be taken to, if we did not want to come back we should write to them, and they would ship everything to us wherever we were. After all, some of these people were our old trusted neighbors, our buddies and friends all of our lives. We thought we knew them so very well, after all, we, our grandparents, and parents had grown up with them, and we felt confident that we would be able to trust them. Unfortunately, since we had no choice in the matter, we left almost everything except money, jewelry and what each of us could put in a knapsack and suitcase which was mostly food, some clothing, jewelry and a few heirlooms. Everything else was left (in hopes) that when we returned after the war we would get it back, but in reality we did not believe we would ever see our home family, relatives or friends again.

I considered myself very lucky because with my blond hair I looked more Aryan than most Christian kids, but it did not help. In reality the harassment by our neighbors and fascists was, only because I was born a Jew.

Somehow I was able to elude them many times, although I was rounded up a few times in Budapest, but somehow I managed to run away again and again. After a while the hostel where I stayed free in Budapest was shut down. My brother Ben, who also lived for a while in Budapest, had been taken several months before I came back home to the Hungarian labor camp, Munko Tabor. I feared for everyone in my family, especially my parents, brothers and sister, so to avoid being arrested in Budapest, I came back home. Soon thereafter, our village was surrounded.

Before we were rounded up and taken here to the ghetto, our hearts were shattered, we were positively scared out of our wits, and very confused to say the least. We did not know what to do, whom to trust, or what to believe anymore. A year or so earlier I went or run away to Budapest, the Capital of Hungary, to get away from the local hate mongers our neighbors, the fascist. After a while there they started to arrest Jews in Budapest people that were not born there. Because of having to elude arrest a few times, the constant fear of not being with family, and then arrest and deportation really frightened me.

So I came back home in time for the Passover holiday, (which is when Jews celebrate the exodus from Egypt) and that's when we were arrested and imprisoned along with other family members. This happened soon after I returned home, (even though I left home because the Hitler Youth harassed me every time I went to and from school or the synagogue) and because of the many problems I encountered in Budapest. I had to leave Budapest to return home for fear of being arrested because I was not born there.

I arrived just before the Passover Holiday. However this was not a joyous holiday for us, like in previous years. As usual in spite of our problems, we had to clean our homes and remove all vestiges of "chometz" bread, or any remnants of foods and dishes that were not especially prepared or koshered for Passover. The house had to be free of "chometz" and special preparation made all, dishes and utensils had to be koshered for Passover.

Besides the harassments and Jew bating by the SS and "Einzatz Groupen" Hungarian soldiers, we were also being assaulted more often by the Nazis, our neighbors, especially the Hitler Youths. I had to run away a few times because every time we left our home for the synagogue, school or food, it was a prelude to an end of a decent life for our family and most the Jewish people in our area. As Passover was ending they came with a loud speaker Hear Ye-order from the Gestapo. All Jews without exception must get ready for shipment to interment. I shall never forget that dismal last day of Passover, when we were arrested and forced to leave our home for the ghetto.

That time in 1944 is forever burned into my memory. The last days of Passover were still very cold in our village and the sky was dark, but we had to be ready for the exodus not our oppressors, we ate our last meal at home. Mother and Father tried to console us as the Hungarian Zondarmed under the SS command, which was not the first time pounded on our door at 5:00 AM, waking us up in a state of panic shouting "Yude Rous!" They told our father they needed good tailors in Germany and ordered us to quickly pack our bags and assemble outside in the center of our village within five minutes. Again, they told us that someday we would or could return to our home in peace if we so desired after they defeated Russia and the allies.

Our father was told that if he and the rest of our family would only cooperate we did not have to worry, nothing would happen to us. They assured us that we would be fine and we would be permitted to return soon after the war would be over, which would surely be soon because Russia was about to surrender then the rest of the world would capitulate to Germany. If we so desired, we could return to our home and be reunited with our family and friends, or have our brothers who will hopefully be let out from the military labor camps join us if we were happier in our new place in Germany or where ever they will take us from this terribly over crowded temporary shelter.

We were awaiting the Russian Army any moment, because they were so close. Unfortunately, we had no alternative. We could not and did not have the means, or the ability to protest, resist, or fight for the right to stay in our home nor to run away; we had become a non-entity. There were very few able bodied men available to resist the Nazis, even if it were at all possible. As I stated before, first our father, then the other older, mature Jewish men 18-45 including our older three brothers, Fillip, Ben and Bernie, had been taken away by the Hungarian Army to Munka Tabor labor camps. Very few mature Jewish men were left at home. Only those of us of the male gender too young for the labor camps, such as Bill, Sam and I, were left to take care of the family. So when the Hungarian Zondarmed and "SS" gave us only a few minutes to pack and get ready to assemble in the village square we were helpless. After all, we were now considered only undesirable Jews. They kept screaming at us (Raus, Schnell Yude) faster Jew. Achtunk if anyone of you are thinking or trying to escape, you and your family will be shot.

To pack took only a few minutes, but it felt like a lifetime. After all we were leaving here our hearts, our home, most of our belongings, our former friends and neighbors, but most of all several generations of history. The "Einzatz Groupen," the "SS," Hungarian "Zondarmed," and local Nazis lined us up armed and ready to shoot us if we disobeyed once we were in front of our homes. They ordered us to march forward to the center of our village.

They gave us no options. Their vicious loud voices "Far schtukene Juden" ("stinking Jews") and loaded guns pointed at us, held all of the authority they needed. We all did as we were told, if we did not obey it would have been considered an insult and we would have paid for it with our life. We knew by then what these people were capable of, especially with the full and enthusiastic cooperation of our neighbors and Hungarians. They knew every Jewish family living there, and after they counted us and made sure we were all there, we were marched past the church which was around the corner from us, and taken not too far from our village to what they made into a ghetto that was on the outskirts, yet close to the adjoining city of Munkach. Most of the local people especially the neighbors were outside watching sort of glad to dispose of us, as the SS soldiers and the Hungarian police rudely forced us to move fast. It will always be a puzzle to me how our neighbors could watch so apathetically, so nonchalantly, to not protest or do anything to help us. It was beyond our comprehension how they watched as the soldiers engaged in these evil acts against their neighbors and old friends without any word of protest, sympathy, or showing human feelings for us, their neighbors, friends and people we were very close to. One of our father's friends came over and told our father to give him for safe keeping our cash, Jewelry and other valuables he will take care of it till we get back.

Besides being a cold dreary day, the hateful looks of the neighbors was scary. We were taken to an old brick factory that used to belong to a prominent Jewish family which, of course, the Nazis had confiscated and converted into a ghetto. It had indeed proved to be a temporary gathering place on the road to hell. The brick factory was somewhat isolated from the population, and was surrounded by electrified barbed wire, we thought mainly because it was close to the villages and the city. They chose this location for the ghetto because the railroad tracks were located in the middle of it, which made it very convenient for the SS to uproot and assemble Jews here from all over the region to be shipped away by rail.

The location was also desirable for the SS because the City of Munkach, which contained tens of thousands, a majority of which were Jews, and the surrounding villages, were close to the ghetto where the Jews could be easily guarded then to be shipped away. And as we discovered all too late from here, we were to be sent to the extermination concentration camps. Of course, we somehow hoped in spite of our misery that we would be able to stay here close by, or to go back to our home soon until the war was over and that we felt for sure we would soon be liberated by the allies. We heard rumors that Russia was defeating the Germans getting closer and closer to us and the other allies were victorious on every front and especially the American and British forces are making headway in defeating the German army.

As soon as we arrived we knew how we were deceived, it appeared that their first objective in the ghetto was to degrade us, humiliate us, and above all, to make our lives miserable. It became very difficult to act as a family. Certainly there was no privacy and absolutely no way to practice our strict Jewish way of living, eating or praying. It was very difficult, especially for our parents and other religious people to practice our faith. No words could comfort our parents' terrible pain and anguish. Especially when we saw how rudely and viciously they treated babies, woman, elderly, pregnant women and the crippled. I just could not tolerate it, but unfortunately I was helpless to stop it.

It was obvious once we got here that their promise to relocate us to a decent place was a blatant lie they concocted just to deceive us. However, it was too late for us. We could not do anything about it even before we were brought here, and we certainly could not do anything about it now. There was no place in the ghetto for us to sleep, no roof over our heads, no real or meaningful jobs, no food except what little we brought with us. Real fear and awful scary feelings started to set in. They warned us if anyone tries to escape will be killed. Now we had no doubt that the worst was yet to come that our nightmare was just beginning. We could not fathom the poor conditions of life ahead of us, special curfews were imposed, but it busted our hopes what the Rabbi told us that the Messiah was on his way.

There were absolutely no accommodations, no housing at all for our parents, three brothers, our sister, for our aunts, uncles, many cousins, or any of the hundreds of other Jewish people, especially the babies, pregnant women, and elderly, from our village, and other villages and towns arrested and brought to the ghetto. And they kept bringing in hundreds more people daily from the surrounding villages and towns. Of course there were absolutely no bathrooms, showers, toilets, or kitchens as promised to us. There was not even a shelter or roof over our head to protect us from inclement nightly chilly weather. It was early spring but the night air was still very cold, and the icy rain at night was not uncommon. It was humiliating not to be able to wash even our faces, and sanitary items for the women were non-existent. There was no provision for cleansing ourselves or for washing and drying clothes, and worst of all nowhere to sleep, and we were running out or food to sustain us. It was so painful for me to see our parents as well as the many little infants, babies, and elderly being exposed to severe inhumanities along with the extreme cold weather at night. Unfortunately, there was nothing we or any one of us could do to alleviate their pain and suffering we tried to console each other. I was still a young boy, but here I sure grew up quickly.

My family was one of the first of many to arrive in the ghetto. We found out that the filthy brick baking oven would be the only thing to provide a little shelter at night for us. So, we removed the bricks and cleaned it a little of the ashes and sod to accommodate ten to fifteen families. Almost one hundred people, were crowded in this miserable small old brick baking oven which we were lucky ones, we used it as shelter to protect us from the night cold. We, the fortunate few, were able to lie down in the remaining ashes or sod to cushion our bodies although it was impossible to sleep. At least the brick oven enabled us to have a roof over our heads and sides to protect us from the cold wind at night. Unfortunately, there were only ashes or sod and no wood or anything to heat the big open tall chimney, but our meager shelter was better than nothing, the other new arrivals did not even have a roof over them, even in the bitter night cold.

After the first few days of ghetto confinement, food was running short, as we hadn't been able to bring much with us. It was beginning to be a real problem for all of us, especially the babies, children, elderly, and of course the overweight people who were used to eating a lot suffered the most, and the pleading and cries for food went unheeded. To make matters worse, after a few days bedlam started to break out. The elite, formerly well off, people were pleading for food just as we were. Only a few days ago they had money no doubt, much of it went to Swiss banks, also connections, prestige and much more food than they could consume, as well as other luxuries more than most of us, now they were paupers in desperation just like the rest of us. There obviously was a terrible shortage of food for all of us here more than ever; even before they took us away from our homes to this ghetto. But at least I was amongst fellow Jews, not Jew-haters.

Friday arrived, and we could not go for the ritual bath or get ready for Sabbath. We did not have Sabbath candles for mother to light, but our father and a few others found a corner to start the Sabbath prayer, mostly with quit mumbling and tears. Then we wished in an inconspicuous way a good Sabbath.

Even if a person had money or other valuables hidden their shoes or clothing, (if not elsewhere) there was no food to be purchased. No one, not even our former friends or neighbors who did not become Nazis, were allowed to come close to or visit us. The guards were afraid they would bring us food or other items such as guns. We waited hopefully and prayed for a miracle, that some of our former friends or neighbors even if he joined the SS or Hitler youth, would wake up their heart and bring us some food or a miracle will happen maybe the war would be over and we would be liberated from this miserable place. But our hopes were shattered and soon realized that we had to become tough, and learned to expect nothing. We were still under the illusion that some of our former neighbors or friends would come to visit us especially at night and bring food or clothing to throw over the wall, or sell us some food or warm clothing, and some were able to do just that, but not too often as the guards would confiscate it or if caught even arrest them.

We were always looking for a glimmer of good news, or a miracle, (any moment maybe the messiah will come) that soon there would be an end to our troubles. That the hate for us Jews would cease, that we would be liberated, and that the war would be over soon. We just wanted to get back to our homes and to a normal life with our family. We wondered how much longer we, as humans, could endure. We just wanted to be good humans, good citizens, and good neighbors, and to be able to practice our faith. In our family we were taught to help each other and others in need, our parents and grandparents were very charitable, but now we were not in a position to help ourselves, let alone others.

It was in the ghetto that our real humiliation, heartaches, and troubles really began. In addition to the German soldiers, we were suddenly guarded by former friends and neighbors! They truly were good people before Hungary took over our area so did fascism took over our former buddies, who had first joined the Hitler Youth, and had grown from Hitler Youth into staunch "Nazi SS" men and officers. What made it so inconceivable and painful to us was that these boys and their parents, who were our old friends, were the same people who were at one time Left-wingers of communists during and after the communist revolution.

Now that Hitler and fascism was the "in thing," and because they were Schwaben of German descent, they not only volunteered to help Hitler's fascism, but took part in it enthusiastically! They became proud German military or Right-wing Nazi extremists. How these same people could switch completely from communism to become fascists, criminals, murderers, and fervent nationalist Germans is beyond comprehension. Even more shocking, why were they even more vicious to us than some of the other German "SS" Gestapo, or even the Einzatz Groupen who were specially trained Jew Killing Units? We learned quickly and beyond a doubt that the Germans were masters in concealing their true purpose in what they were trying to do to or with us.

It was amazing how successful the Germans were in attracting hundreds of thousands of collaborators as we found out later not only in our area, but also in Italy, Romania, France, Poland, Ukraine, Galicia-Lithuania, Hungary, Slovakia, France, Greece, even in occupied Russia and other countries. The

Germans also enticed many leaders of religions and diverse nationalities to advance their ultimate Fascist aim. Their intended goal, as was stated by Hitler, was to create the pure 1,000-year German Reich to dominate the world. This was to be known, if Hitler succeeded, and our Schwaben were sure they would triumph as the pure 1,000-year Reich of the German Aryan super race. By then even the local Germans boasted that they intended to control not only Europe, but the entire population of the world. They felt and acted superior to everyone else, even the adjoining villagers who were Ruskie, as though they were the chosen elite people emanating from the pure blooded German race that was destined and must rule the world for at least 1,000-years.

Even while in the ghetto, they still wanted us to believe that we were just being relocated away from the local Jew hating anti-Semites. In addition to that, they told us again that we would be taken as soon as possible a greater distance away from the actual fighting front. They boasted that for sure, soon, they were going to defeat the communist Russians and their evil empire, as well as Britain's Royalty. They also boasted that it was only for a short while that the American capitalists, or any nationalities or races that could stand in their way of complete world dominance would be eliminated.

By this time, after being incarcerated in the ghetto for a few days, we had no doubts what Hitler and his collaborators intended to do with us. We got now the feeling that they were gathering all the Jewish people first in the ghetto, and then probably disposing of most if not all of us. When it was too late, we found out that their intent all along was to dispose first the old, the sick, and the very young, and then use us the young, strong people as slaves. We started to realize by the way they treated us that when we outlived our usefulness, they would kill us one by one, and rid themselves and the world of Jews. They threatened to kill all of us if anyone of us would try to escape.

Each day and hour in the ghetto was more miserable than I ever imagined, it seemed to drag on and on; each day felt longer, more difficult, dimmer, and darker than the previous one. Yet, somehow, because we had no choice, so we tolerated it. At least we were still together as a family, not all of us, but at least as a partial family which was a blessing. Our mother, father, brothers Bill & Sam, Sister Rosalyn, and I, along with several of our uncles, aunts, many cousins, and our Jewish friends and neighbors, were all cramped together in this old brick factory. It was miserable ghetto subsistence, even if only for a short while. We also had no doubt that our other uncles, aunts, and cousins who lived in the other villages of Lavik, Vary, Davidkiv, Unternshlos, and other areas, would soon be brought to this or other ghettos. We had no idea if they would be transported here or where they might be taken to. We did not even have a clue where, when, how or why we were here or where we were going to be taken away. We were petrified of what was in store for them and us.

We sensed more and more realistically the real precarious danger we were in. We understood enough German to get the meaning of the comments we overheard from the German guards, as they talked amongst themselves when they thought that they could not be heard or understood. In some cases, the guards actually wanted to be heard and boasted amongst themselves as to what we could expect. The few days in the ghetto were very long and frightening. They, in effect, discussed amongst themselves that this is the beginning of the end for most of us.

Even in this misery, we were still somehow sure that the world was still populated somewhere by decent people, like the ones we used to know, not like the inhumane people that they changed to and we were now exposed to. We wondered, and were very scared what the future held for us or for that matter for others in the world, be they Jews or Gentiles.

We had many questions, but no clues or any idea as to what might be in store for us. The guards did everything to make our lives miserable, even the little children and the elderly were not spared. Even at our young stage in life we were forced here to age very quickly into maturity. Even before we were shipped out of the ghetto, the guards did not let us rest; they constantly came up with new schemes to make our lives unbearable.

We slept very little because we had no beds, mattresses, or covers. The rough concrete or soot floor, along with the sod or coal dust, we had to breath was very hard on our bodies and lungs. They also worked us very hard all day. The guards created jobs out of meanness and spite just to make us miserable, and maybe to keep us from becoming restless or to just cause us trouble because they felt like it. The weather was still very cold, especially in the early morning and late evening, but it was getting warmer even a little hot during the day, as a result, people became sick with influenza, our lives became from bad to worst.

There is no doubt they wanted to weaken us, especially our spirits. They had us move, by hand, the piles of large rough industrial bricks that were stacked up on one side in the brick factory. We had to throw these very rough bricks to each other without gloves, catch them with our bare hands then throw them to the nearest person in line who was about eight or ten feet away. In this way, our group moved the large piles of brick from one side of the ghetto to the other. When the bricks were stacked up at one end, the guards would order us to move them back to the other end, and so it went on all day, moving the bricks from one end to the other to make our life more difficult.

Because we had to throw and catch the cold rough bricks without gloves, our hands soon had no skin left. Our hands were raw swollen and skin torn after just a few hours of catching and throwing the large heavy rough bricks we had very little skin left. As a result blood would drip first thing in the morning from our hands over the frozen ground, then thaw during the day. If we dared to slow down or stop, we were flogged and hit with sticks or rifle butts by the guards. This was repeated day after day hour after hour over and over again. Sometimes our hands were too tender or too slick with blood to catch the bricks, but we did not dare slow down or drop the bricks. We knew what to expect: if we stopped, even if we had no skin left on our hands they would have beaten knocked us down or even worse trampled on our head and their loaded rifles with bayonets were ready for us.

The ghetto was not isolated, every day we saw people going back and forth to work, but none of them made any attempt to help us. This misery for us was "entertainment" for the guards; it continued for as long as we stayed there. No wonder our previously strong, 48 year old father was beginning to look old and weary after only a few days in the ghetto. We hoped that this frail look on his face was only temporary, not, God forbid, because he might be physically ill or that his worries for us were getting the best of him. As a caring father, he was exhausted from work, but mostly he was concerned very and worried for us, fearful for our future, for our safety, and indeed he must have had a gut feeling of the danger to our very lives. Our Uncle Yosef, our mother's brother, tried to calm us but was unable to contain our Aunt, his wife, whom we called Pimchu, who was scared out of her wits and showed it.

Our stay in the ghetto reached about fourteen days. We found that during this night, cattle-cars were brought in on the railroad tracks apparently designated for us. We were told that we were being sent east to work in Germany, by now we did not believe it, but what choice did we have? Most of us were exhausted, hopeless, and sick. I heard an SS man scream at one of my friends that he will make him crawl on his hands and feet, then shoot him if he does not carry out the orders quickly and properly.

Early the next morning before daybreak, they woke us up screaming and cursing: "Schnell, Raus, Schnell Yude raus!" We were ordered to assemble promptly for counting. After everyone was accounted for, they started loading us and jamming us into these cattle cars, just like cattle but tighter. Obviously, we were petrified. The SS guards continued to scream "Yude Schnel." They were laughing as they cussed at us, and whipped us in an effort for us to move faster. They jammed us into the cattle cars like sardines in a can.

We were not prepared for our miserable trip, no matter how hard life had been under the fascists the past few years, or in our village when I had to run away or in the ghetto, when they started jamming maybe 80, 100, or 120 of us into these small cattle-cars. By then we were without food or water for what we were afraid was going to be a long journey. There was no room to breathe, even if the cattle cars had little windows and slats with barbed wire over them, we were unable to turn or to sit down, let alone lie down to rest our weary bodies and certainly nowhere to sleep.

They locked and bolted the sliding doors from the outside to make sure no one could escape. Worst of all we had to idea where we were being taken to or how long the trip would take. Finally, the train began chugging along ever so slowly in contrast to the racing of our petrified hearts. We were hungry, thirsty, frightened and hot during midday, but cold at night. We learned that the train ride was going to be even worse than the ghetto and who knew what's awaiting us.

The train stopped and started many times switching on the tracks. At each station our train stopped a long time to make room for other trains to pass, especially military trains. It seemed we were heading in the opposite or wrong direction from time to time. Certainly people our neighbors and others that saw us through the cracks must have felt our anxiety, our fear, and helplessness, but unfortunately they did nothing because they did not care to help us. Our strong father, who was always very strict with us suddenly pleaded with me many times, calling me "Yankele," (my Jewish name) telling me again and again "no matter what, I want you should live." He made me commit myself that no matter what, I must stay alive. I am sure that he said the same thing to brothers Bill, Sam and sister Rosalyn. My father repeated this to us, and ordered us to stay alive many times, and it was very strange and frightening to me since our very strict father never asked us twice to do anything, and never repeated himself. Now he begged us and got us to commit ourselves to hold on to our life no matter what.

My angelic mother just looked at me, and told me to please listen to father and make sure to do what he tells me to do. Her eyes looked frightened and petrified, and her demeanor said it all. We were packed so tightly that there was not even room for the young mothers to breastfeed their babies. There were no bottles in those days, so the babies cried and cried waiting to be fed, which was very disturbing and agitating to all of us. We tried to turn our heads away, so as not to embarrass these young religious mothers as they had to breastfeed their infants. After a few hours, the elderly could not stand on their feet, and we could not hold onto them, so they just collapsed. There was shoving and pushing as we tried to protect the heads of our elders. People were screaming crying and pleading for help especially at the people standing at the railroad station or bridges, but no one listened to us, there was no help to be gotten. The people we saw at the railroad stations, on bridges, or when we stopped for hours in the country at roadsides just watched nonchalantly as we pleaded mercilessly for food and water. Very few people cared or responded at all at least I did not see any human response.

Things soon got worse after a few hours; the younger boys and girls needed to go to the bathroom, and since there was no way to move, they had to urinate in their pants or on the people next to them, people were throwing up, vomit was all over the car. This brought on screams, cussing and outcries, and created more pandemonium. As time went on, the stench got increasingly putrid, especially during the day when the sun heated up the car. Each hour was like days and the problems did not end, fleas were infecting and eating away at us. This trip dragged on and on for what seemed like endless painful long days and nights. These few days in the slowly chugging along cattle car felt like an eternity.

Little did we realize that we were soon to arrive in the worst hell on this earth. After several days and nights the train stops sometime after twelve o'clock midnight at its final destination and we just stood there freezing all night, waiting for daybreak, we noticed the sign "Arbeit-Macht-Frei," meaning "work makes you free." A terrible stink penetrated our nostrils. Finally, in early dawn they opened the locks from the outside and started again to scream at us "Yude Rous, Schnell." For most of our people it was not only the end of the journey, but the end of their lives. The rest of us were to endure here unbelievable sufferings, and the worst inhumane treatment in the annals of human history.

The stench coming from the tall chimneys greeting us was awful. Little did we realize that it was the smell of human flesh, from our brethren, and family being burned by the thousands in the crematoriums each day. But what we learned and were forced to endure upon our arrival in Auschwitz Birkenau cannot be described or comprehended in the human mind. Uunfortunately we found out soon that no matter what we endured in the past, our misery was just about to begin. The conditions here became harsher and harsher almost daily and it got worse by the hour and minute.

We also found out after the war that less than two months after they took over our area from the Hungarians in March of 1944, 38,000 of us Jews were sent from our ghetto alone by cattle cars to Auschwitz. My family and I were among the first to be shipped out of the Munkach ghetto.

The world watched as the Nazis killed 75% of European Jewry. We must ask ourselves, how could they remain silent and apathetic? By July 8th, 1944, 476,000 more Hungarian Jews, mostly from our and other nearby areas, were shipped by cattle cars to Auschwitz, that's where they took us supposedly for work or really for extermination.

Chapter 4: Buna

After being so inhumanely processed upon our arrival when we were deported and brutally transported in cattle cars, squashed in like sardines, from the Hungarian ghetto (where my childhood and our home was taken away) brought first to Birkenau-Auschwitz I where, after being brutally and inhumanly processed, they began to cruelly divide us; who shall live for a while and who shall be murdered right away by separating us who shall go to left, who to the right, and who shall be sent straight for immediate death in the gas chambers, including children, elderly (including our Father), retarded, gay, and any others that did not fit with their ideology for slavery.

The reality of the death carries problems that have not even yet penetrated my mind. I just could not look at these grotesque looking people with striped clothing. They assigned us young, strong, healthy ones for slave labor. First they sent us to the main camp of Auschwitz II. From there I felt fortunate because we were assigned after only a day or two to one of the sub-camps.

Very soon we were again screened after standing in the morning cold at attention for hours, we were checked out by our tattoos, and then ordered to line up (we had to jump) onto the awaiting open trucks to take us to that assigned camp called Bunaweck, (Buna) Monowitz, formerly Polandin upper Silasia, also known as Auschwitz III. It took only a short time but it felt like an eternity to get there. Just like Auschwitz I and II, where I was processed, the new camp was also surrounded by a double row of electrified barbed wire, high fences, the tall well dressed SS guards with high boots and their vicious German shepherd dogs were all over us as well as they were walking between the electrified fences 24 hours a day constantly on the lookout for someone of us in striped uniforms who might be trying to escape. We were also surrounded by tall watch towers with bright flood lights shining on us with the guards and loaded machine guns aimed and ready to shoot at us all day and night. The guards that were close to us had either a gun in hand a cudgel or whip ready to unleash their proud Fascist viciousness or anger at us, and of course, a loaded pistol on their side holster ready to shoot us with or without reason or provocation. After a while, here not only was my youth taken away, but for a while my beliefs in a just God or human decency were utterly gone.

Once we arrived inside this camp of Buna, the early morning was still bitter cold, we found out that our misery is going to be in full swing as we were ordered to jump down from the trucks quickly, which were emptied of all their slave labor prisoners and human cargo. The SS and Kapos venomously screamed at us and beat those of us that did not jump down and line up fast enough to suit them, as we had to be counted again by our tattoos. No matter how fast we moved, it was not fast enough to suit them.

We were surrounded by vicious Kapos with green triangles, which meant vicious criminals and convicted murderers. They were assigned by the SS to oversee us, warning us if anyone steps out of line they would be killed, or would wish they were dead. They also told us we would never get out alive from here because the gas chamber ovens were close by. Here our new sub-human existence really began. Our vicious treatment left us haunted by our hunger pains, especially when I was remembering the hearty breakfast with homemade bread and other such luscious meals, made by our mothers hand, a tall glass of milk from our cow, tender love with proper care. Now, our hunger pain as time went on was unbearably awful, and slave labor has never in human history been so unbelievably exploited and utilized so brutally anywhere in this world as it was here in Buna.

At first we thought of how lucky we were to be assigned for work yet not to be guarded and abused inside an electrical and electronic warehouse. How lucky I felt to be able to think at first of these SS and Kapos as soldiers or normal human beings, performing their duty. They were dressed very prim and proper; in fact, some of them were very handsome.

After a while here, I also wondered if the people in charge of us were regular Germans, or Nazis criminals but above all I questioned if they were really humans or killers, murderers or just plain viciously inhuman even though I was extremely petrified, and feeling lost.

I was very scared, but I could not help thinking out loud that hopefully our Father, Mother, five brothers and our precious sister were strong young and healthy, as well as our Uncles, Aunts, cousins and friends. Surely I was hoping they would be OKay no matter where they were. Most of all, I was hoping they would be liberated by now. My encouragement ensued as I reminded myself of the fact that they were young, strong, healthy, and would surely assigned for work and be OK somewhere here or close by.

We soon found out that we were brought here for hard slave labor to facilitate several of Germany's largest manufacturing companies purely for deriving profit, as well as to keep its Nazi economy prosperous and above all to keep the war machine going at a high pace by using us as free slave labor so the Germans should be able to control the world soon.

The terrain of the camp and factory was fairly flat, but the area was surrounded by mountains and forest. The city of Auschwitz was close by and the larger city of Krakow was not that far away; but at that time we had no idea there was life or a city nearby.

These large prospering companies, such as I.G. Farben Industries, Krupp, Mercedes Benz, etc., are still going strong, even in today's Democratic Germany, and indeed throughout the world.

When we arrived in the Buna, we saw a similar sign on top of the entrance into the camp as at Auschwitz I and II, which read, "Arbeit Macht Frei", meaning "Work Makes Free." However we found out how deceitful and what a farce it was. The trucks that brought us here shuffling back and forth between Buna III and the main camps of Auschwitz I and II, probably ten or twelve times a day, and some people were marched from Auschwitz I and II to this camp. These daily trips brought between 1,500 to 2,000 healthy, young, strong men here alive for work, and they took approximately the same amount of emaciated weaklings and mostly skinny dead bodies back to Birkenau-Auschwitz for cremation. The bodies or corpses they took back of course smelled awful, they were stiff or mostly skin and bone.

After being in Buna a few weeks most of us were more or less dead. Our comrades bodies were thrown, without compassion, just dumped onto the trucks in the same manner as one would load wooden logs. The guards forced us prisoners out of the trucks, then had us later load the dead bodies on them. The German guards and Kapos had absolutely no feeling or emotions and neither did many that became Nazi collaborators and fascist drivers who took our peoples bodies to Auschwitz-Birkenau I to be dumped into piles to await cremation.

We noticed quickly that the only freedom the fascists guards or Kapos gave us from here in Buna was our death through slave overwork, (at least ten to sixteen hours a day) plus getting beatings, painful punishments, vicious treatment, starvation, outright murder, or death by disease that engulfed us here. To the elite Germans, especially the industrialists, we represented free slave labor. They did not care what they did or saw, and they totally ignored the inhumane treatment we received, the fact that we had hardly any food to sustain us, how much a we suffered from the beatings we got day in and day out, even if we only lived a short time. They were confident they could get fresh healthy young new Jewish slave laborers free when and if they need it.

We were immediately assigned to a barrack and work detail; about 1000 of us were crammed into each of the small barracks, which were designed to house only 50 to 100 people. These were un-insulated, windowless, shoddy, wooden barracks, very rough wooden bunks three to four tiers high, instead of beds, with thorns sticking out of rough wooden boards, no mattresses or straw to sleep on, nothing to cushion our infected, weak, aching, bruised bodies after a grueling hard days work, being batted around, and no type of covering at night. It was still cold in April and May but not even a sheet or blanket was available to cover our cold bodies. The reality of being in a death camp has not completely penetrated yet but the horrible truth was nibbling at me, and I was getting more scared by the second.

The horrid smell was all around us, not only from the dead or dying but soon from our unclean lice-infected bodies, it was awful when we walked at night into the barrack; it was really unbearable. There was no air circulation or any way of cleansing yourself, and the others around you were also filthy and smelly. Even if you wanted to keep yourself clean and healthy, you were out of luck. Sweat from hard sweaty slave work is not all that pleasant to smell but by the evening, especially in the summer's hot weather, it was unbelievable. Lack of bathing facilities or any way to wash or clean yourself was terrible enough, but we had no clean changes of any clothing so the stench was even worse; a truly unbearable acrid stench, and one that my nostrils could not and will not ever forget, even if I live forever. I did not have the capacity to imagine how horribly I might have smelled. After all, I was wearing day in and day out the same cruddy clothing without being able to wash it. It felt like it was almost glued to me. We were hoping and counting on the Russian or any allied army getting closer to liberation.

Each group or barrack people was assigned or created for a specific work detail in this huge I.G. Farben Industry and we had different assignments to quickly and efficiently complete. Our barrack group started working very early the next morning in the adjoining Monowitz I.G. Farber Industry, each day or even hour was unpredictable as to what work we would be assigned to perform for our task masters. All orders had to be adhered to instantly and unquestionably, which made us revert to a child or it could be a testimony to the human instinct of self preservation and hope.

Many times they made us haul large heavy concrete blocks a long way with our bare hands, into the building where we lifted them up to a platform to build, inside the warehouse, thirty foot high dividing fire walls. We had to build several of these wall dividers inside each of the huge warehouses that we worked in and we worked awfully hard and fast because these buildings contained highly sophisticated electric gauges and other equipment. These walls acted as a buffer to reduce the damage in case of bombing of that building by allied planes, or fire from sabotage. This way only a section of the contents in the building would be destroyed instead of all of the valuable merchandise in the huge warehouses. There were many sophisticated tools we stored in these and other nearby buildings, such as gauges for anti-aircraft guns, tanks, airplanes, etc., for the military, as well as items for German civilian use.

We would constantly be pushed to work harder and faster; sometimes sixteen to eighteen hours a day. Most of the men in my barrack were assigned to work in these large warehouses, which were warehousing I. G. Farben products, as well as other buildings that served the elite German industries, which even manufactured railroad cars and other heavy equipment or anything else needed for Germany and its allies in their insatiable desire to conquer the world.

Time for us just kept dragging painfully on and on; so in order for us to help defeat the Fascist and shorten the war, as an example, we managed to sabotage a lot of these electronic gauges by knocking out the quicksilver, thereby making the anti-aircraft guns useless against the allied bomber planes. One time they caught some of us sabotaging these tools because they found some of the quick silver in a garbage can so some of our boys were hanged that day in the center of the camp. We were forced to painfully watch as our friends and bunk mates were hanged, the guards did not even cover their heads when this was done. They wanted us to witness the full affect of their brutality so that we would a lesson and know what we would face if we violated any of the master race rules. It made it so much more painful to see these hangings held in the parade ground, "Apel Platze," with everyone of us watching. How painful it was to be marched so close to these friends, people we worked with and see them dangling by the neck on a rope. Yes, we got the message that death could encase us any moment. Nobel Peace Lawries Prof. Elie Weisel, who arrived about the same time in Buna as I did here described some of his experience here in his well written book, "Night," but there really are no words that could describe the sufferings and constant abuse we endured.

Other work often assigned to us in the long hard hours work days, included digging ditches by hand with shovels and picks, working on the roads and railroads, especially repairing the damages done by allied bombs, repairing or getting ready loading the railroad cars, trucks and heavy military equipment rolling as they were shipped or moved from the factory to the battlefields or confiscated goods sent to the interior of Germany.

The I.G. Farben Industry was also one of the major producers for military hardware that kept the German Army supplied with the best war machinery and armor available then on the continent. At first when we were brought here, to us it looked as though the German Military might be invincible, later American and other allied military ingenuity got seriously involved in the war effort to defeat fascism by bombing and crippling their factories, railroads, and their lines of supplies, which was the pivot in halting fascism from taking over the world. We hoped and assumed no doubt it was because the American people wanted to save us so they pushed the politicians which was the main thrust I believe that the U.S. finally got serious to defeat the invincible mighty German army.

In addition to the SS guards, the people in charge of us, such as the foreman and other managers, were mostly German, but the Blockelsters and Kapos were inmates also; they were mostly condemned German, Polish, Lithuanian murderers, rapists or other hardened criminals, as well as some Jews wanting a little extra food and other breaks, such as better shoes, clothing or even better sleeping quarters, maybe also a blanket. Most of the time they woke us at 4:30 AM for breakfast, we got a cup of what they called coffee, at noon if we were lucky, a bowl of soup that contained very few calories, and after they checked us out by our tattoo in the evening, a ration of what they called bread, which was mostly sawdust, and maybe a little soup.

Unfortunately, these Kapos wanted to show off for the SS, how rotten they could be to us. They wanted to look and some were more vicious and mean to us, even more than some of the SS guards. The Kapos lived in our barracks, especially the Blockelsters, who were in charge of the barracks, but they had better quarters, a little more food and few other perks or privileges; such as getting less abuse from the guards or Kapos, or just a smile, which was forbidden to us.

These gestures were all right with the German SS as long as these Kapos and Blockelsters brutalized us, and threatened us constantly, and painfully, I remember some were even more vicious than the SS. Other Kapos, especially ones in charge of our work, they were just greedy mean people who simply wanted some extra food and got their frustrations or meanness out their systems by being mean to us. In addition they got better food ration, a little better clothing (that was removed from the dead), and other favors they might receive, such as not getting whipped so often.

After a while in this horrible place many of our fellow inmates just disappeared through frequent selection for the crematories or just simply died of starvation, exhaustion or diseases. Normal life for us in this camp ceased and our world turned into chaos. I was hoping that the hollering and cussing at us would subside now that we were in the work camp under their complete control, as we were promised by the Germans before they took us from our homes, especially now that we were assigned to a German factory and camp for permanent slave work. Unfortunately, as time went on the unwarranted uncivil screams got worse. They vented consistent rage and hate at all of us. The Kapos made sure that we complied fully and completely to the daily rigid task master labor rules and regulations, assignment designed for us by the Nazi German government, we learned quickly that its puppets were just as bad or worse, especially the Fascist Ukrainian, Lithuanian, Kazaks, Polish, Slavic, Hungarian as well as other collaborators who also wanted to eliminate us Jews from the world just as badly or even more than the Germans, if not by gassing when we arrived in Auschwitz they wanted to make sure we would be eliminated soon through hard work, starvation, abuse, and disease here in Buna (Auschwitz II).

If we were lucky we got some coffee or tea in the morning. The main meal at noon we were supposed to get a liter of meat soup four times a week and vegetable soup three times a week, unfortunately we did not get meat, potatoes or cabbage which it was suppose to contain and the bread was suppose to be 350 grams plus margarine and jam. Unfortunately we only got 1,000 calories a day, when we needed at least 5,000 calories a day for the heavy work we did.

We were constantly reminded and never allowed to forget that we were not in Auschwitz just as prisons or criminals; that we were in these camps for annihilation, liquidation, and they were not going to make it easy for us. They made sure that first and foremost we had to suffer and work every ounce out of ourselves till we could not function before total eradication. Hitler and his cohorts, including the German bosses, foremen, Kapos, Guards or the "SS" overseers wanted to make sure the entire world, and us especially, understood that they wanted to wipe us Jews off the face of the earth then take control over everyone. The collaborators were from many ethnic backgrounds and nationalities who became fervent fascists when Nazi Germany wanted and was in the process of succeeding in conquering the world. They had Polish, Hungarian, Slovak, German, Ukrainian, Yugoslavian, French, Lithuanian, and Slovak, Greek, Italian and others. Hitler attracted enthusiastic very loyal followers, especially the young, for his criminal activities. These people were excited to be part of trying to conquer every part of the world, especially its people. They had followers even from the Arab countries, as well as America. The Nazis wanted and almost succeeded in Europe, then to take over the entire world, but first and foremost to conquer all of Europe.

Every morning the Blockelsters and Kapos in charge of us would awake us at 4:30 AM with screams, "Raus Jude," then we had to jump out of bed, post haste, and since there was no bed to be made or clothes to put on, (since we slept in our one and only clothes, there was no time needed to get dressed) we had to hurry to assemble on the Apel Platze and stand lined up, five in a row, at attention for a long time sometimes for head counting. The SS did this by checking the tattoos on each of our exposed left arm no matter what the weather was like.

Many times getting out in the morning the person bunking next to me was dead, just stiff. He could have died from disease, which was rampant amongst us, such as diphtheria, phemphicus, typhoid, etc., plus starvation, beatings, abuse, or many other things that caused us pain or reasons to give up on life. We had to be very cautious to preserve our energy, as every second counted in our determination to cheat death.

We had to be very careful with our meager ration of bread. I learned quickly that I had to break off a small piece of bread at a time, and let it dissolve in my mouth slowly to make sure it would last a long time then store the rest of it inside my shirt which was tucked in my pants held up by a string. One time I was awakened by a rat trying to nibble at my bread which was tucked against my body in my garments, or course I was not the only one bothered by the mice and rats, they had a feast at night, especially nibbling on our dead comrades' bread or bodies.

In the summer months they would make us get up early dawn (probably at 3:30 or 4:30 AM). Since there were no clocks anywhere, and we had no watches, because they took from us watches, jewelry and all other valuables when we arrived in Auschwitz, we could only guess at the time. We had to be outside at the assembly ground within minutes of being woken up, for roll call, and checked out by our tattoo on the left arm. Since there was no shower or running water in the barracks they concluded we did not need time to bathe nor did we have clean or any other clothes to change into. No doubt we looked like something out of horror pictures because we were starting to feel more dead than alive.

In the winter months they would probably have permitted us to shower in special shower places, but if we had the showers we were afraid to do so because we would have frozen to death on the spot when we got outside in the miserable freezing cold weather. The horrible freezing Selasian mountain temperature would have made our thin threadbare cotton uniforms freeze and stick to us. We did manage to wash our faces and hands when ever we could during the wind, with the snow and ice. Also we could break up a little of the ice to put into our mouths to quench our thirst. The winter weather was especially harsh on us in this mountainous and swampy area, sometimes reaching 10 to 20 degrees below zero, with winds up to 25 miles per hour when we worked on the outside. In our miserable weak condition, it felt like 100 degrees below zero, and the freezing weather was not much better indoors. We had no windows, insulation, or heat in the barracks, or in the warehouses where we worked, and of course, working in the outdoors was awful. Unfortunately it was a very harsh, icky reminder of the pain we endured when I visited the place even fifty years after liberation.

Unfortunately by now, six or seven months later, we were more dead than alive and the cold weather made it feel so much more painful from hunger, thirst and injuries we suffered as though that was not enough pain inflicted upon us going to the toilets was an added misery having to sit on the rough cold stone toilet made of stones, mixed with concrete we had to sit round those holes 50 to 100 people had to sit at a time in a row, it was drafty with only gas and putrid smell coming out of us because we did not have good digestive food within us.

During the extreme heat or cold the SS had the civilians go indoors and they made us "Katzetniks" (condemned people) work mostly outdoors, and have the Kapos keep an eye on us, especially in the winter, and the only clothing we owned was what was on our body, the thin cotton pajama-like striped torn uniform that we were issued when we arrived in Auschwitz-Birkenau, and of course, we were without underwear.

If that was not bad enough, we were many times forced to stand at attention before daybreak or at night outside on the Apel Platze (parade ground) sometimes freezing for hours with our bare left arms exposed till the SS called and checked out our prison number that was tattooed on our left arm and also sewn on the left side of our uniforms. For some reason, when it was cold the wind was especially brutal to us tearing away at our frail bodies. But I continued to look and search for family, friends, relations or anyone I could recognize.

The SS men and other collaborators stayed indoors in bad weather as the Kapos and Blockelsters, for the most part, who were also condemned men did their dirty work for them. It didn't matter what the weather was like, be it cold, raining, or snowing, we had to be out and stay at attention until everyone was accounted for, dead or alive. The people who were not accounted for on the Apel Platze were usually accounted for and taken dead from the bunk and thrown outside into a pile of dead bodies to be picked up by trucks that took them to be cremated. Each day between ten to fifty men (fellow inmates) in our barrack alone died at night and wound up amongst the pile of dead people. After a few months in Buna if our people did not die from starvation, then from overwork, being beaten, shot, hanged or they succumbed to the many diseases that plagued us. When the body wore out, the soul had no choice but give up.

We also found out years after liberation that many of our other fellow inmates were killed by the medical experiments which the Germans performed on us unknowingly (or knowingly to very few).

Unfortunately, some of our people in this camp just gave up trying to stay alive because they could not take the suffering anymore. It was easier to give up all hope, especially when a close relative, a son, a father, uncle, cousin, or close friend died in their hand or next to them in the bunk. It was very painful to see your loved ones unable to move because there was no life left in them and there was nothing any one of us could do to help them. I was absolutely petrified because I could not be with, or see my parents or brother Sam, even though I discovered he was in this same camp. I noticed more and more people all around us were more dead than alive marching close by or bunking next to me it made me realize that probably I did not look much better so I grasped what father meant when he made me promise that no matter what trouble, fire or near death, I must stay alive; to survive.

They worked us very hard, at times ten to sixteen hours per day, sometimes seven days a week. In addition, when we were returned to the camp, they made us stand at attention again on the Apel Platze for a long time to be counted and rechecked by our tattoos to make sure no one had escaped or hid in the factory or in a railroad car; alive or dead you had to be accounted for at least two times a day by the SS.

Vermin and disease had become so widespread amongst us that the SS, the foreman and guards got worried about their health, not getting to close to us they surely did not want to catch or be affected with our illness. The guards must have been disgusted at themselves, and bored with the misery, horrors and tragedies they put us through so for more fun and joy, the SS designed and set up hanging parades, picking their victims at random, or other ways to punish and torture us, on and off the Apel Platze, or parade grounds. Most of these horrific things of course took place on our holy days evenings or on Sabbath again and again. We had to stand for hours to watch our friends being hanged, and left dangling for hours. Then they forced us to march past them. They came up with crazy accusations, announcing that these people were planning to escape or did not salute or properly obey the commands, any excuse to amuse themselves. For us it was very painful, and beyond human comprehension that we were forced to look at our dead friends dangling from the ropes on the gallows.

At times we were made to watch for hours as a warning to us not to try to disobey their command or plan any escape. They proudly concocted ways to announce some excuse as to why those people were hanged just to keep us constantly scared and worried. The hangings were not enough to satisfy some of the SS so they continuously came up with new forms of killer entertainment to amuse themselves at our expense. They did not have to have a reason to punish us or to hurt us; they knew we were constantly in pain. Sometimes they would pick randomly a few of us to beat and chase these young boys so that they would be forced to run towards and into the high power 1,500 watt electrified fence guarding us. The German guards would watch with pride to see how high the electricity would blow or throw a boy, of course when our boys touched the wire, this of course would kill him.

Another group of SS would sometimes bring in especially trained German shepherd dogs and have them attack us between our legs, tearing our man's vital parts out. As I am called upon to recount these and other horrific events even now, fifty years later, I cannot believe these German SS Guards was part of the human race, supposedly created in Gods image. (Most of them probably disappeared t North America, South America, the Arab countries as well as Canada; pretending to be innocent human beings).

One time I had the ill fated misfortune of witnessing the guard ordering some of our people to pick up a young boy about my age and toss him into the air and the SS took bets among themselves on which one of the SS guards could or would shoot out his right or left eye before he hit the ground. Another time I witnessed an SS man get his jollies by removing ears because he claimed the boy did not hear him good; they would even cut ears from living people to see who had the largest ears just for fun. These horrible things were done in full view of all of us in certain sections of the camp or even in the parade ground (Apel Platze) those who would dare turn away, not to look would become the next victim, that person was selected for the next round of brutal SS entertainment for themselves maybe to torture or killing just for kicks. To say some of them acted savagely would compliment them. Some of them just were outright vicious plain inhumane torturous murderers, and each time something so bad occurred I was horrified beyond description why and how could a human become so inhuman? As a result I started to get a feeling of helplessness because the future looked so bleak just like a dog caught by dog catchers.

We were asking ourselves the question, "Why had God embittered our lives so cruelly?" He took our Jewish ancestors out of Egypt from slavery, now it is so much worse for us than it was for our ancestors. Had we Jewish people sinned so much more than before or do others not sin? Why were we Jews who are supposed to be his chosen people, always put in danger by rulers, conquerors, kings, or dictators?

There was no escaping for us from this hell on earth called Buna, no way to get away from the fate of the oppressors that engulfed us. Somehow, no matter how painful it was, I had to set aside my feelings, unfortunately, I had no choice in the camp but to endure the agony and tortures that engulfed me, which were beyond human comprehension and in spite of that I held onto the slim hope that maybe the Germans and Nazis would soon be defeated by the allies, and that maybe real soon we could survive this hell on earth and be liberated before it's too late for the rest of us and the world.

I wanted to survive most of all because I promised my parents that I would try to stay alive, no matter what, but enough is enough. I suffered long enough to remember the past horrors without giving up hope for a better tomorrow. I felt obligated to hold on, not only for my generation; but for our religion, all religions, nationalities, races, creeds, and humanities hopefully to avoid genocide. For other people, I also wanted to survive to be able to see and be reunited with my family, to be able to love again, and a chance to live like a human being.

For some reason the people in our section or barrack in Buna were exposed to some of the most barbaric horrendous brutality imaginable sometimes even more than the others interned in other sections; here we endured some of the most barbaric inhumane acts that were meted out in our camp or anywhere on earth.

It might have been because a lot of Kapos and Blockelsters assigned over us by the SS were of German and other Aryan extraction and were formerly convicted murderers or condemned hardened criminals. Because they enthusiastically did the dirty work, and because of their meanness they, of course, were given extra food ration, sometimes eating in front of us to make us suffer more from our hunger pain, they also had better beds and favors by the SS, thereby becoming even more enthusiastic torturers and doing the SS dirty work even better. We feared them just as much or more than some of the guards.

We were petrified when some young SS man would come into our section of the camp for fun and personal joy to show us that Germany and its people were invincible and beyond human caring or feeling, such as making us throw a young boy into the air so he would catch him with a bayonet on his rifle which unfortunately ended up sticking through his young frail boys body. When I saw this I wanted to die, and be taken out of my misery quickly but I remembered my commitment to my parents, so I was somehow able to hang on. Our Jewish lives or mainly others meant absolutely nothing to any of them, only their joy of proving that Germany's leader, Hitler, his Fascist edict and cohorts, ruled over everything including God, and indeed the entire world's humanity.

We had a very dreary looking harsh woman come into Buna our camp similar to Elsa Koch, who was the SS commander's wife of Buchenwald (where I was liberated). Elsa was known as the "bitch" of Buchenwald. This SS woman was known as the bitch of Auschwitz; she would come into the camp and make us stand for hours lined up on the parade ground, Apel Platze with our bare arm sticking out with the branded tattoos showing. She would make us stand there sometimes for hours, no matter what the weather was like even in the bitter cold, as she selected young boys my age to step forward to make sure the skin was the right color she picked and wanted that day for her lamp shades, handbag or other items.

One time I sadly remember, she picked boys in front of me, the side of me, and or in the back of me; somehow I was spared, I do not know why. Later their hands or arms were whacked off with a large sharp hatchet-like knife, and the skin removed just so she could have lamp shades or other leather goods made of the matching color of young human skin. All that mattered to her was that the skin colors blend properly for lamp shades that had visible tattoos on them. Some of these lamp shades and handbag creations were found later in Elsa Koch's and many other German's possessions, when the allied forces liberated us in Buchenwald. Those perfectly matched lamp shades because just one more proof of the most brutal unusual cruelty ever performed in the world by people against us fellow humans.

We saw occasionally the Nazi hierarchy, visitors or even guards who would sometimes take photographs inside the camp with great pride the atrocities which they were participating in or watching being performed against us. I overheard them bragging by brazenly saying to each other that these photographs were intended to show off to future generations of an extinct race, as well as use it as a threat on others what would become of them if they did not fully cooperate with Nazi Germany. There is no doubt if the Nazis had succeeded, after the war was over they planned to show their children and grandchildren these photos and brag about what they had done to this inferior extinct race of Jewish or other people. The guards probably told their young children when they were home how they would first rid Europe of the Jews and were indeed going to eliminate us, then concentrate on riding other inferior people such as the retarded, gay, gypsies, Slavs, Polish, Greek and others, from the face of the earth. They took great pride in their criminal, inhumane acts which they did to us, as well as others. How could they otherwise have a compelling motive for their inhumane savage acts performed against innocent kids, elderly, women, retarded, crippled, gypsies, and other; with such enthusiastic pride and get away with it for so long.

After the fifth or sixth month in this camp, each day when we came back after a grueling 16 hours of mind boggling hard work, after a very fatiguing day we realized that our survival was nothing short of a miracle in itself. We literally collapsed on the rough wooden planks which was our so called beds, from total exhaustion but too tired to sleep. Those of us who were still able to get out of bed in the morning and work in the factory knew that the only way to stay alive was to overlook and endure all the suffering. Just to keep going. Not to think, period. Especially about the pain, hunger and our insurmountable other problems.

No matter what humiliation, no matter what pain starvation or disease we suffered, we forced ourselves to go on marching military style in cadence; no matter how painful it was to drag ones foot in front of the other. We tried to just keep on going and somehow made it because we had to. We had no choice but to give the appearance that we were in good enough shape to work, even though hour by hour and day by day it got more difficult for us to move our limbs to put one foot in front of the other. No matter how painful it was, I kept looking for and hoping to get a glimpse of brother Sam or other family and loved ones alive.

We could not let the SS or their collaborators in charge of us notice any injuries or see how sick or weak we really were. If you did succumb and showed your frailty, your pain or any injury you had, then you were their target for that day or the next to be disposed of. They would have immediately shipped you back to Birkenau-Auschwitz I, to the gas chambers and crematorium without any hesitation. So we just continued to work hard in our emaciated condition no matter what the mean SS task masters ordered us to do. Since we had no choice, we tried to ignore our pains, our hunger, thirst, heartaches, and sufferings; we worked very hard controlling ourselves just to get through another minute, an hour, a day or maybe a week. In fact, we realized that the hard slave work helped, it took our minds off of our many hunger pains; injuries and other sufferings.

When I gathered the strength in my eyes, I was able to take a real look at the guards and people in charge of us just to see if they could possibly be real humans because I did not and neither could anyone of us believe humans could be such vicious animals. When I looked at them, how well they were dressed, well fed, and in good health, in spite of that, I felt a little pity for them. Somewhere, somehow, unfortunately, for them and us, they had lost all traces of humanity, empathy, dignity or the ability to care, and certainly they had lost or relinquished all trace of their decent humanity. No matter what their origins were, how good a mother or father they might have been born to and reared by, it was certainly changed by Hitler. Germany's Fascist thirst for world dominance and in their insatiable desire to conquer the world's people, this turned each and every one of them into sadistic torturers, monsters and criminal murderers. The Kapos were so brutal with their whips and were even more brutal when the SS were around.

When I recall the vicious way we were treated here in this God forsaken place called Buna (Auschwitz III) and there is no doubt probably in the other Auschwitz sub-camps, the Nazi program for the final solution to the Jewish and other ethnic people was almost brought by them to fruition.

We had to salute the SS men by Caps off then Caps on ("Mutzen auf, Mutzen ab") we never marched or worked fast enough to please the SS. There is no doubt in my mind that had the Nazis been able to go on with what they called their final solution of Jewish problem, it would have also brought the end of what we got to know as our civilization.

The Germans were great inventors of destructive weapons, poisonous chemicals, cyclone "B" gas, as well as rockets to destroy cities and its people, with which they aimed and bombed London, England. They also developed and were ready to produce the atomic bomb, and other military hardware, for their planned destruction of what we refer to as decency in the human spirit and most of all their conquest of the world. What might they have invented next had they been given the time for the destruction of the entire human race? Had they been permitted to go on, there is no doubt they would have used atomic bombs with their rockets, and other destructive armaments in such a way mainly, God forbid, to end all life.

We all know now that it was Germany's Nazi philosophical insanity to rid the world of all inferior races, especially people that were not pure Germans; all others were to be enslaved first. We know, without any doubt that they would have successfully annihilated first the Jews, then they would have annihilated next maybe the Gypsies, Slavs, British, or they would pick on a race, nationality or people of other religions one at a time, then one world's people after another; without regard of human dignity; who knows then maybe their own people would kill each other.

There is no doubt in my mind that the end of civilization as we know it probably would have occurred had they succeeded, if their conquering of other countries and nations had they been allowed to go on, unabated, if the allies had not stopped them.

To the Nazis in this Buna camp, we the Jews, were non-human, an excess disposable entity. They thought of us and others as vermin to be rid of. We were sure when they disposed of us Jews it was only a matter of time as to when or who would follow next for destruction, maybe the Russians, Czechs, French, British, Muslims, Gypsies, the Slavic people, they proved it in Russia and Czechoslovakia when they felt like it the entire townspeople were wiped out. After all, they could decide who or which people were undesirable and who or where is to be disposed of by them, and of course every time I got a beating I felt the pain, degraded and very low in spirit.

One thing in this camp was sure, beyond a shadow of a doubt. They wanted to destroy us. The Jews at first here because no one stopped them. Those of us that somehow managed to live, just to hang on through each minute, hour, day, or night wondered if it would be our last. Not only I, but most of us stayed awake each night wondering if I would ever see my beloved parents, brothers, sister, uncles, aunts, cousins; I also wonder if I would ever see our village again, the wonderful Jewish people, and our non-Jewish neighbors and many friends with whom we grew up before we were taken away to this hell on earth.

I was also afraid to fall asleep at night because they used to give us bread when we arrived at first every day, then every second or third day, approximately one-half pound or so, of bread even though it was made mostly with sawdust or sand, you had to treasure it; you had to hold onto it to keep you alive, and if you fell into a real sleep the person bunking next to you might take it from you thinking that you were dead and did not need it. So all night most of us stayed awake and held on to our precious little bread tucked under our garment, and you also guarded your canteen and spoon (which I tied with a string onto my pants) all night we held onto it for dear life as I lay there listless. I had to be aware at all times what was going on around me in order to hold onto these two precious possessions because if you lost your canteen and spoon, you could not have received next day the soup or water which even if it did not contain a lot of vitamins it was like manna from heaven when given to us a day, two or three days apart.

Lying in my rough bunk squished in at night with all aches and pains with lice all over eating away at me, and the pain from sores inflicted on us from beatings, bumps or infections, left an undeniable impact on me. Often whilst in pain I thought of my wonderful kind caring grandfather, Moishe Aaron, our mother's father, whom I only knew slightly as a child with his rugged broad shoulders, white long beard, generous heart and large happy eyes. He was living with us, he made his livelihood working with horse and buggy and he was a very devout religious Jew. I remember him with a never ending smile on his face, and I vaguely remembered our grandma's good hearted sweetness, even though I was very young when our grandparents died, I have very fond memories of them. I hoped they were now in heaven hopefully looking after us. Now I was happy that they had not lived to see their children and grandchildren brought to this horrid slave camp for extermination. I was also glad that my tender loving grandmother had not lived to see our names taken away from us and replaced by a number tattooed on our left arms.

It is our tradition that Jewish mothers and fathers name their new born children after someone beloved in the family whom they lost, or a boy after a pious revered Rabbi, because there were so many boys in our family I was named (Jakob) Yankele, after the baker, a neighbor across the street that passed away.

In a way I was thankful in my misery here in Buna that our grandparents died peacefully before the Holocaust engulfed us, at least they were buried beside each other in a Jewish cemetery just outside our village before these fascist took our area over and engulfed us. I was glad to know that they did not have to suffer because they were such wonderful humans and good Jews that they were no doubt in heaven and safe from these horrors. It would have been sheer torture for such righteous, good, loving people as our grandparents to see their God-fearing religious children, fairly religious grandchildren, and other loved ones tortured, humiliated, and slaughtered just because they were born, raised, and lived as Jews. It would have been impossible for them to endure such unjust torture that the right wingers thrust upon their siblings. They had such unbending faith in God and pride in being Jewish. They and their children were, along with our parents and brothers, good workers, good neighbors, and good humans. Most everyone in our area respected and liked them, Jews and gentiles alike. Now here in Buna I was only a number, not part of humanity.

Most nights I could not or did not dare sleep because I was too hungry, scared, tired, being nagged by lice, sick, or trying to forget about my hunger pain. I would invariably think of my beloved parents. I had no idea where they were. I wondered if they were alive and doing OK, and what about my brothers, the oldest one, Fishi (Filip) whom I looked up to. He was the first to be taken away and drafted to the Hungarian (Munka

Tabor) Labor Camp. Next was Benjamin (Ben) who was also drafted after living for some time in Budapest, the capitol of Hungary, where I also went to when I was trying to get away from the local Hitler youth in our village. They also took my frail brother Bendi (Bernie) to the Hungarian labor camp. I was worrying and wondering where brothers, Berish (Bill), even Smilku (Sam), who was in the same camp with me. But we were forbidden to be in the same barrack, work detail or be associated with each other. I obviously worried most about my younger sister Rajziko (Rosalyn) who was cute, tall; mature looking but so very young, only 13 years old. I was very worried for her, how or would she be able to take the suffering and live through such brutality they were dishing out to us. The last time I saw her was in Auschwitz I, Birkenau the day after we arrived she was with mother when we were marched out of the camp. I was hoping they were alive, together somewhere.

I also remembered and longed for our uncles, aunts, and many cousins that I had not seen since they took us away from our villages, and our homes, first to the ghetto, and then to Auschwitz and now here in Buna. Wondering and very concerned as I was laying restlessly tired, hungry and in pain, what became of them as well as our many relatives and friends.

In my insomnia, sometimes I even worried about our American relatives, Aunts, Uncles, cousins, whom I had never met, and wondered if they were still alive. I was glad they were not caught in this inferno. Wondering if they were aware of what is happening to us, their family. I was glad that they had immigrated to America years before, because if they had not left Europe many years ago they would have been also (God forbid) caught in this abyss, suffering with us, or worse, and as lost as we were in these extermination camps. Contemplating if they really know of the fate of their brothers, sisters, our parents, and their extended families brought to Auschwitz this hell with us.

We certainly did not know, nor had any inkling, if they or anyone was alive. I had no clue as to where they were. If, God forbid, Fascism had taken over America, what were they doing? If they, too, had been able to make it through like me just one more hour or day as we struggled to hang onto life. My greatest and best hope was that our wonderful uncles and aunts in America were alive, and by now well informed of our family's plight, so they would arouse the American people to get going, hurry up to defeat the Fascists of Germany, Italy ad their allies throughout the rest of Nazi Europe, as well as Japan, their collaborators. I kept on wishing and whispering to myself that it was high time for the Americans to step up the war efforts to stop this Nazi murderous insanity before it was too late for all of us, them and their American families. All of us, especially our family, worshiped our wonderful U.S. relatives and they were really our only hope, if any, to a normal life, in the future, when and if we, praise God, come out alive from this inferno.

In a way I was glad that our brothers Philip, Ben and Bernie had been taken away, by the Hungarian Nazi's, to the "Munka Tabor" because they were of military age, to the Hungarian forced work camps. I hoped that they had not suffered as much under the Fascist Hungarians as we had to suffer under the Germans and that by now I hoped and prayed that they were safe and had been liberated by the Russian or other allied Armies. I thought about and worried about my frail brother Bernie often who was also taken to a Hungarian military labor camp, I wondered if he would make it, as well as our two oldest brothers, Ben and Filip. Would they be strong enough to endure whatever they were exposed to? I certainly hoped so but most of all I hoped that they would be freed by now.

Here we were struggling more and more each day to make it, another hour, another day, another week; maybe we can try to hold on for another day, week, or month. Because by now our physical and mental condition was so bad you could not expect to survive more than a moment at a time. I knew that unless I was able to keep my mental equilibrium, my physical strength was going to disappear. The SS men came often early morning and late evening through our camp for selection of the weak Katzetniks, or Muselmen. We had to stand or march past the selection officers naked as they noted the tattoo on our left arm, picking whom they considered too weak or too old for the hard work they demanded from us, people whose numbers they noted on the list were shipped the next day to the gas chambers, then for cremation. Unfortunately by now, my body was stripped of muscles and fat but I was determined to cheat death. Each time they did these selections, we hoped that any day now the Russians or other Allied Nation forces would liberate us while they were in the process of defeating the Germans.

Painful memories unpleasant thoughts played tricks on us, while it was not too long ago that Brothers, Bill and Sam, and sister Rosalyn, Mother, Father, and I were brought in cattle cars from our home and ghetto to this God-forsaken hellish place called Birkenau-Auschwitz, then Buna III. I shall never forget being squeezed into the cattle cars (like sardines) brought to this place of destruction, not only to our human bodies, but most of all our spirit and soul. Especially the uncontrollable and torturous mental pain and anguish I felt when I arrived, and now that I have been here in Buna, the Auschwitz III camp for awhile. I know why people could not hang on to life too long here especially without the ability to withstand suffering so much from hunger, abuse, and slave labor day in and day out.

Every day as we went to work early in the morning to this humongous industrial complex being marched in cadence from one place of work to another, standing for re-assignment or to be counted by your tattoo on the Apel Platze when going or returning from work camp. In this camp I was always on the look out for my father, brothers, uncles, cousins or friends. (There were no women in this camp)And I had no idea where the male or female members of my family were and this troubled me greatly because people were dying all around us.

After being in this camp a while as we were on our way back from work, a miracle occurred, a voice startled me; I recognized the voice of my brother, Smilku, (Sam) as we marched past one of the other groups of the camp I was absolutely elated the first nice thing that happened to us since I arrived here. Sadly we were in different sections of camp, and barracks, but what a relief for my aching eyes and shattered heart when I recognized him; he was the best sight for my sore eyes and the best medicine for my heart. Despite the terrible way he looked, and the danger to my frail life, just knowing that Sam was alive and in the same camp gave me some desperately needed hope that I craved for to help me survive even if it was from moment to moment at least one person from my family was alive here and hopefully we will be able to see each other on occasions.

Now that I had found at least one brother, Sam alive, it gave me more incentive to live, I had gained a new purpose in my life. That purpose was soon to see him again, if not today then tomorrow, if not tomorrow, then the following day. Even if I would only be able to glance at him from time to time my spirit was ignited; hopefully there was a chance that I might see him or be with him soon. This gave me something to look forward to especially in the evenings and in the early mornings. I could hardly believe my eyes; it was absolutely wonderful every time I was able to glance at him. It bolstered my spirits that hopefully all or at least others in our family might also have survived this long, just by chance maybe others were alive here in this camp or close by; but most of all hopefully they were liberated by now. We were hoping and praying that liberation would come to us real soon before any one of my family perished as I have seen my comrades here with their relatives dying fast. I thought about this hope coupled with fear many times each day. As time dragged on, hunger, pain, and suffering became worse, and hope and critical time became more precious.

After a few months of so much suffering, I did not have the strength to go on. I felt that to give up now would be to let the fascism and evil triumph over me and humanity, also to give up hope, would be to destroy the love and faith that my angelic mother and strict father had in me and as we brothers had in each other. The responsibility that the forefathers, especially our grandparents, instilled in me, that somehow no matter what I had put up with or endure I felt I must survive. Yes, I still had faith, even though at times it was faint, that the spirit instilled in me would help me live through this. No matter what happened or what I had to endure. I felt that I must keep my promise to my parents to survive.

As my heart pleaded with the Almighty: please do something to stop our suffering, after all have I not suffered enough? "Genik is genik!" ("Enough is enough!") I also prayed for survival, not just for myself but for every one of us in the camp. I prayed for all religions and all humanity as well as members of the Jewish faith, especially for those of us in the concentration camps. I tried to adhere to the traditions we learned as children in Hebrew School, and which was handed down by our forefathers from generation to generation and practiced by us for over 5,000 years even before "Moses" time when the Almighty gave us the Bible.

As children, we placed our faith in our elders and the Almighty. There is no doubt in the camps after having to endure so much suffering just because we were Jews, some of our people began to doubt our tradition, faith and even doubt the existence of a God or at least we felt he turned away from us just like he did at first in Egypt, but then with an outstretched hand, he took us out of Egypt. We felt it was time for the Almighty to take us out from bondage and suffering. Yet most of our elders even in camp near death had such a deep faith in God that they kept praying silently and felt even if they could not make it any longer in this hellish camp at least some of us young ones hopefully would be delivered and rescued soon from this "hell on earth".

Outwardly we were busy fighting and hoping for survival, inwardly we were scared out of our minds and prepared for anything, including death. By being forced to do the task master's terrible hard slave labor day in and day out it helped keep our minds off the hunger, thirst and other pains including being eaten up by lice that plagued us constantly. Also the agonizing pains we endured was noticed less by us when we kept busy. In fact, hard work helped to set aside our pain to stay alive for the moment. Nothing can ever compare to the pain and agony we endured, especially the worrying about our loved ones, who had been taken away from us hopefully are now free or taken to other camps, hoping that they escaped or were liberated by now. Even better I hoped that they were not incarcerated in this type of torturous camp; because surely it was not an existence but barely hanging on to frail life by a thin thread. But unfortunately father, mother, brothers, Bill, Sam, sister Rosalyn, and I were brought to the Auschwitz Extermination camp together so that gave me real concern, I was petrified for their wellbeing.

Each day or new work assignment for us was a new terrifying experience, whether it was loading heavy boxes into RR cars or trucks of course without the help of forklifts or other equipment or loading of other heavy things onto a railroad car or trucks, or repairing the railroad tracks that were damaged by wear and tear or the allied bombers damaged them. This kind of horrific slave labor we had to perform under the watchful eye of the SS or Kapos has never been thrust upon human anywhere in annals of history.

One of the Elder persons who were close to death pleaded with me to keep my chin up! Keep clean, to ignore my hunger pains, keep working and ignore tiredness, walk straight, look ahead, not to appear as suffering, dying, to look as a muselman, or they will send me to the gas chambers and crematorium.

Day in and day out it seemed as though I was in the real hell on earth or totally in another terrible world. Everything in this camp especially to our group, the SS were so vicious, unbelievable excruciating that there is no words to describe it. In spite of that I kept telling myself that it is just a bad dream or just part of a prolonged nightmare I was having, hoping someone was going to wake me up any moment and tell me its not true that all this suffering, pain, and hunger is not real, that it was just a bad dream, just a bad nightmare, but being awake did not help.

I painfully recall that on several occasions how uncaring it was to some in civilian clothing, no doubt big shots coming to review the camp; they brought a very young looking tall girl. She reminded me of my sister, Rosalyn. I was dumb founded that she watched the cruelties with pride as their German parents and others bragged about them being the master race, and we Jews were going to become an extinct race soon.

No matter what suffering we were forced to endure I was wondering and I could not believe that this could not and should not happen in this world, not in this or any century among Germany and other Europeans who were supposedly civilized normal humans. After all, what do fascist schools teach or their parents tell their children at home about how they were taking part in criminal acts torturing and killing fellow humans, especially children, and communicating such despicable heinous crimes against humanity?

No matter how strong you appeared when you arrived in this hell on earth, whether you had dark or light hair, small or large features, either you were tall or short, your personal characteristics were joyous or sad, those who had been a little overweight quickly became skinny and the tall shrunk terribly smaller beyond recognition in a few weeks.

Unfortunately, soon we all started to look terrible, not only to resemble each other but in a while we all began to look alike. We were referred to as "Muselmen," weaklings. We all had the same skinny unhealthy sad looks that most of us after a few months in this camp. This of course pleased the SS men, the guards, and even the German civilian Plant foreman. This way they proved that they worked the hell out of us so they would get more free healthy young slaves.

If a stronger looking inmate's new arrival was noticed by the Kapo, guard or SS, then this person was given even less to eat than the other, not that they gave us anywhere near enough food to sustain us even when they were generous with the food rations. I do not know how we existed on watered down soup and so little bread mixed with sand or sawdust, and sometimes in the morning watered down coffee, but somehow we did make an hour or a day at a time even though it was for an unbelievable unhealthy sub-standard existence. There was almost nothing most of the time nutritional in the soup or in the bread little sawdust mixed with flour; we had to be mentally strong to help keep up our strength, to hold on to our food ration even to work hard, let alone to stay alive, and the further back in the line you were when a new large barrel or tub of soup was started to be dished out. The few nutrition or vitamins there was in the top of food tub but there was no complaining allowed. To make matters worse, a sliver of fat or spoiled meat might have been floating on the top of the soup, but very rarely were any of us lucky enough to get it. This wonderful delight was slipped to the Kapos, Blockelsters, or their favorite buddies or a boy they might want for sex. We knew that if we asked the server, who was dishing out the soup, for more it would mean more cruel punishment by the Kapos overseeing it. So we gladly accepted the soup given to us or the bread flour mixed with sand or sawdust; we were just happy to get anything to put into our mouths. When one drank water soon after eating the bread, if you could get it, it made the sawdust swell up in our stomachs, giving us a full feeling, but later we would be sick from it causing us sever intestinal cramps. Dilemmas and temptations, especially over the lack of food, terrible weakness were constantly thrust upon us, shaking our conscience. All of us were trying to get in front of the soup or bread line before they ran out of food because our very survival depended each time on that little soup or a piece of bread we got.

Our group was referred to as a heavy construction crew especially the barrack that I was assigned to. Reward for this hard work, if we were lucky, sometimes we were given a little larger piece of bread. I learned upon my arrival, the first day, from the other inmates if you were smart enough you only nibbled, a little piece of bread at a time. This way, the 'bread' would last a little longer, and sometimes it had to last one, two, or even three days.

If anyone of us was hyper, lost his mind, caused a problem, complained, maybe he was just in an off mood, someone forgot to salute a German guard, or when we had to stand at attention for a long time and fainted or lost his composure, the SS guards took it out not only on that person but on a few of us. If the guards just felt like making it worse for us, the food and water were also withheld one or even several days from that person or a group of us. The Nazi guards' theory was why waste food or water on us, the condemned Jew, especially if they had picked some reason to single you out. You would soon be dead anyway. After all, we were here for only one reason; for slave work and ultimately to be eliminated from the face of the earth.

The cold spring is gone. Here we were surrounded by mountains and the camp was in a low lying wetland as a result and the muggy hot summer began to make it more difficult for us especially in the middle of the day. Along with the hot muggy weather, of course, came insects. All kinds of nasty flies, bugs, big rats, and especially lice all over us by the thousands, feasting on our heads, under our arms, and between our legs because our hair had grown back; these are just a few of the pesky insects that feasted on us, which weakened us and spread all kinds of diseases and illnesses among us. Our camp was formerly a swampy area which embodied a breeding ground for the insects which were all over us. I could run my hands over my head, pick lice up to be crushed by the hundreds. Probably our filthy smelly bodies, dirty clothing, along with the unsanitary lifestyle, sleeping barracks attracted them, our bodies' inability to deflect them provided a virtual banquet table for these insects.

To us it felt that the people in the world did not care to save us that therefore, did not want to know that millions of our people were being tortured, starved, and killed. During the summer, especially mid day, it started to get so hot we prayed for rain to cool and hopefully cleans us a little bit, especially when we worked outside with all of the hard work we did outside such as digging ditches, heavy lifting of building blocks, lifting and hauling rock and steel. When we did have the luxury of rain, to cool us a little of course, we stayed outside; it felt so good and we were grateful just to be able to catch the rain in our hands to drink it, and splash some water on our lips, to wash our filthy bodies. Even the guards in their meanest behavior could not take that wonderful pleasant feeling we got from the wet rain. It felt like manna from heaven, especially when the guards were under protective shelter and away from us then we could really enjoy washing our faces hands and heads.

To make matters worse for us sometimes during the heat of the day the guards would wait until the hottest part of the day, about noon, instead of lunch, which we did not get regularly.

They would sometimes have water delivered to us they would permit to give it to a few, but they would wait until the rest of us really craved it and expected it, especially when they say us with our tongues hanging out in the air waiting for it, only then they would pour out most of the water onto the ground. The guards knew how painfully thirsty we were and how many of us had succumbed and died from lack of fluids and nourishment for our weak emancipated bodies. I will never forget the pain when we saw many of our comrades die with their tongues hanging out because their bodies were swollen from the lack of fluid, or what the sawdust in the bread mixed with water did. Soon diseases were breaking out amongst us, most of all because of lack of sanitation, decent food and fluid.

What a horrible sight to see a friend or any fellow human person that arrived in the camp about the time I did, whom you had befriended working with or bunking next to you, or any of our fellow inmates whom you got to know having to give up on life because they had no strength left to keep on fighting to stay alive. We knew our time to leave this hell on earth would also come soon. The guards would delight themselves and laugh at the sight of our misery as they poured water on the ground to be soaked up by the sand and hot sunshine. Even to this day, I have flashbacks to that turbulent time and visualize these horrible; painful sights how fellow humans could be so cruel and inhuman. These and other horrors kept me from sleeping for a very long time, for many years after liberation, even to this day I do not get much sleep when my memory brings me back to that turbulent time.

As the allies started to be victorious and getting closer and closer to liberating our area they started to bomb more often the factory we worked in. As soon as the sirens sounded the

SS and other Germans went into the air raid shelters we built for them. I will never forget one time as the bombs were falling all around us there was, this young former Rabbi who created a sensation as he started praying out loud as he climbed on top of a dirt mound proclaiming loudly as he stood on top of a pile, "The way to truth and justice is often filled with affliction and pain, let us ignore the atrocities and our sufferings, let us pray to the Almighty for deliverance." Whilst we prayed no doubt most of us had a difficult time trying to believe there is a God, after all we have prayed and waited for deliverance to take us out of captivity for so long.

I know the camp had some sort of nursing center. They called it a hospital because it had a red cross on it but very few ever came back alive from there. Most of them that went there were shipped with the piles of other dead bodies or almost dead bodies, to the Auschwitz I crematoria or were used for a while for medical experiments.

The summer was short lived, fall cold weather started to set in, especially at night and early mornings, while this summer days felt very long like many centuries for me, it passed even though painfully somewhat quickly because we were kept occupied with hard work. Somehow those of us that were still able to hold onto life began to accept our fate that it was only a matter of a little time. I shall never forget my sixteenth birthday, September 18th, I considered myself somewhat fortunate to be alive in this camp and know that at least one brother, Sam, was still alive, and in this camp, I saw him some mornings or some evenings on our way to or from work. But now with an early winter on the way it concerned us that it would be even more difficult to make it through the horrible windy, cold days and long nights.

The allies started more frequent air attacks to bomb the factories we worked in. As the bombs were flying and exploding all around us we were of course outside watching as the anti-aircraft guns shooting at the planes which gauges we managed to sabotage luckily so very few planes were hit. One time during one of the prolonged air raids, another young Rabbi stood up on a big pile of dirt and started to pray out loud. He told us it turned out to be our High Holy Day of Rosh Hashanah, our new year. After solemn prayers he told us as loud as he could in Yiddish to ignore the atrocities by quoting again and again from the sages the way to truth and justice is often filled with affliction and pain. He also quoted that our sages were slaughtered many times for the sake of our Torah, God and us. I overheard a comment from one of our boys that if our sages were already victims, why do we have to suffer now so much, the Rabbi was praying in Hebrew from his heart the Holiest psalms, then he ended the prayers he mumbled in Yiddish, "Heavenly Father, please have compassion on us, heed our cry, grant our supplication. Please rescue us God have pity on us." As soon as the bombing stopped, the sirens sounded and of course the guards returned to make us resume our slave hard work to clean up the debris and repair the damage caused by the bombing.

As the weather turned colder especially early morning or towards the evening we gained a little encouragement just because were not so hot and humid with the seat from hard work when the sun was beating down on us and hopefully the lice will stop feasting on us, but fall cold weather arrived, too soon as a result of the windy icy cold went right through us because of our rundown condition, especially on the late afternoons, nights and early morning.

The frequent bombings gave us some desperate encouragement and hope for early liberation. As time progressed it seemed that the war was going against the Germans, the soup with the meager substance and bread was given to us less and less often. However, we were given a little more drinking water, even time was starting to be allocated for an occasional shower or even though it was cold, it made us feel relieved.

It started to get real cold, especially in the late evenings, nights and early mornings. We still had only the same one outfit and wore the same thin torn, filthy striped uniform which we wore during the day and slept in every night, on the hard wooden uneven rough bunk boards. Now as the cold was getting worse, the wind cut through the thing clothing, which had holes in it, like a knife through our weak bodies and we could not stand the driving gusts of wind going right through us.

How I longed to be home again with my family, yearning for decent bed cover, some straw to cushion my achy body, some warm, even hand-me-down clothing that I used to get from my brothers would feel great now. I wanted some long warm underwear, and especially longed for thick socks that our mother knitted to help keep warm my cold frozen swollen feet. I thought of the many woolen scarves and blankets that my mother and Grandmother (may she rest in peace) had made by hand for us, as well as the thick covers on our feathered bed at home. These and other warm thoughts helped also a little to keep my hopes alive at night while lying without heat in the drafty barrack on the rough wooden bunk.

Every day the guards were pressuring us to work harder and harder to accomplish more for them. We worked hard, digging by hand or shovels ditches, fixing the damaged RR tracks so the cold did not affect us so much. And now, winter was fast approaching; we were scared of the cold because we knew how cold in that area it got, but when the snow started to fall we caught the flakes in our hands to wet our thirsty lips as if it were ice cream, to quench our thirst but by now what we really craved was that we should be liberated from our misery hopefully without any more delays.

I remembered when we arrived here, the cold weather was very harsh on us, even though we were still in good physical condition, but we had this thin striped suit; we feared the fall and were petrified of the winter because we had no good clothing to keep the chill out, or strength to fight it, especially while standing sometimes for hours in early morning and late evening on the Apel Platze as they checked us out by our tattoo numbers and working in the gusty winds under the taskmasters on the outside was absolutely miserable. It was not pleasant to see the SS and most of the guards had high leather boots, thick uniforms, warm overcoats, underwear, ear muffs, and hats; whilst we had only the original issue skinny striped torn uniforms.

The winter days, nights, weeks, and months seemed very long as though they would never end; it was unbelievably brutal on us; I felt surely that soon it would also be my end but I was encouraged to keep going especially when I was able to catch a glance in the camp of my brother Sam marching by me. One time late in the afternoon while I was working with concrete blocks, one of them had ice on it and my fingers stuck to it. I was afraid I would lose my finger but somehow I was able to pry them loose. One time I was punished by a Kapo so hard he knocked me down then he began to kick me till I got worn out, there was nothing I could do but get up and go on as though nothing happened.

After the hard cold day's work, then at night laying down without blankets, mattress, or straw on the cold, harsh rough uneven wooden bunks was awful; it made our infected sores more painful. There was absolutely no heat or insulation in our barracks. We slept up to 7 people in a bunk section which was approx. 8 ft. long and 8 or 9 feet wide and 3 rows of bunks on top of each other. It was really overcrowded, but at least being so close to even a half life human body that had a little warmth kept some of us alive because even the warmth from another half-dead body resisted some of the chilly wind; which made us feel a little warmer but in spite of the cold the lice kept feasting on us.

Each day and night was getting more difficult on us especially in our weakened condition, and if you were assigned to the upper bunks you hardly had enough strength to climb up or down three tiers of bunks and you had to do it quickly in the morning or for a late night roll call. We were always concerned about the almost daily selection, being picked as a Muselman if you looked expressionless, defeated, with no hope because you would be next to be picked to be shipped to the gas chambers and crematoria.

I did not realize it then, but I sure found out later that one of the Kapos' favorite joys was to kick us in our leg because he saw an SS man kick me hard and others with his big boots. Once I was kicked very hard so I was in excruciating pain and limping not thinking that I could have a broken leg from this SS man's big boots hard kicks. I found out years later in England after a soccer game why I had so much pain, never before realizing or giving a thought to why it continued to hurt so bad. After they took an X-ray in England, I did not wonder anymore because they showed me the breaks in my foot. Who knows, it could have happened on any of those or other occasions when I was kicked by the SS man but I did not dare show to the Kapos or SS that I was hurt or it would have been the end of me. I could have surely been sent next morning to Auschwitz-Birkenau for the gas chamber and cremation.

As winter approached faster, we felt very cold, even more so because of malnutrition, and our terribly weak condition if that was not enough, the close by Szilezian Mountains of Poland, where Auschwitz III and Buna sub camp was located had terribly cold winters, especially the winter of 1944. Some days we would have to break through the ice just to be able to work to repair streets, rail road tracks or other damages caused by military vehicles or allied bombings.

By November the roads and most water were frozen up to a foot deep, but we had to work on them just the same, repairing roads, working on RR tracks, or repairing utilities, especially after the allied bombing raids which became more frequent as winter approached. Many of our comrades lost their feet and lives because our feet froze on to the ground, not only because of the cold, but mostly because of our weak, undernourished, diseased condition and we had to stand still on the Apel Platze for hours. The extreme cold we endured caused the loss of fingers and toes of many of our comrades. My toes and fingers were painful for years, even to this day due to frost bite; this pain continues for many years to this day I suffer from arthritis. There was nothing we could do to keep them or us warm. Of course the diseases amongst us killed our comrades like flies and most of us became Musselmen, weaklings, but miraculously somehow we were still existing in our disabled weary bodies even though our minds were without hope or ability to express or tolerate our pains, but hoping the SS would ignore us or we would be victims of the next selection to be shipped away for eradication.

Those of us who somehow managed to survive till these winter months survived mainly because we refused to give up. We expected and hoped the Russians or other allies would liberate us any moment. Of course we hoped for a miracle, per chance to be free again or soon liberated before real winter gets here, then hopefully survive, recover then hopefully get well to see spring again.

We dreamed and hoped that spring would get here soon, any minute, and most of all, in our delusions we dreamed that we would soon be liberated because fortunately the allied bombings were becoming more frequent. Hopefully by some miracle we would see ourselves as free humans, watching the green grass growing again and that it would be the time for renewal of faith and seeing the budding of flowers along with the fragrant smells of nature's beauty, and most of all, to see and be with our beloved mother, father, enjoy our brothers, sister, our many relatives, and friends that I missed terribly and of course a good nutritionally healthy meal would be a life saver.

But here in Buna the unfortunate brutal reality set in. Even in the cold weather, we could smell the stench from our own body and the dead or near dead bodies around us, especially those dead bodies stacked in piles outside. Even this far away from the Auschwitz crematoria when the wind blew our direction, we were able to smell the smoke from the burning human flesh at Birkenau, Auschwitz it was an awful horrible stench. In addition, the constant smell of decaying flesh all around us, from the dead bodies that were stacked along the sides of buildings and in open areas. They were supposed to be picked up early in the morning to be taken to the crematoria for burning. We knew that they would rot if the sun would come out even in the lukewarm, vicious winter. In spite of our misery, we mumbled to each other about a better tomorrow.

Most of the time fellow prisoners, people around me groaned or cried from hunger pain or injuries they received from many things; especially the beatings, diseases, sicknesses, broken bones, open sores, many of us were subjected to 25 lashes publicly if we did not please them, naturally the hundreds of lice we continuously feasting all over our bodies especially on head under arms or between our legs and they did not rest, therefore we could not rest even at night, no wonder we looked like zombies. We were also exposed to raids at times by the rats; some were as big as cats that came from the out-houses trying to nibble at night on our bread or our toes. These rats were too friendly to us so we tried to chase them away. One time I caught one rat by his tail but he got away with a part of tail remaining in my hand.

It was getting tougher and tougher to stay alive so naturally some of our people tried to take themselves out of their misery and give up because they could not take anymore the pain, hunger, and suffering that was constantly inflicted on us. Some tried knocking their heads against the wooden bed post to end their suffering. Although there were many attempts at suicide, only few succeeded by hanging themselves with the string that held our pants and cup up; somehow we managed to talk most of them out of it, giving up on life, especially after suffering for so long we were able to convince most of them that hopefully we would be liberated soon.

By now even when our oppressors let us sleep, we were too tired, hungry, sick, or scared of what the next hour or day would bring to interrupt our restless or sleepless nights. I recall lying in my bunk, which of course I shared with others, thinking and talking of heartaches I had caused my parents as a kid or young boy, and regretted all of them. Especially the times I refused to eat good hearty food made by our precious mother's hands that she cooked with so much love. Just because of my childish stubbornness or because I didn't like something. Or when I grumbled about being forced to wear hand me down used clothes I did not like because they were handed down from my older brothers. Or, failing to please my strict and Orthodox father going and learning in Hebrew school, and especially pleasing my grandparents, in observing the Kashrus, strict Sabbath, or pleasing my older brothers with work that I was assigned to do because I wanted to do something else, like to play soccer with my friends, but reality had to return in this camp the misery and suffering continued. We had to get up very early go to work in a hurry no matter how weak or cold we were.

Almost daily we heard many warning sirens and anti-aircraft guns going off and most of all rumors that the Russian troops were near by or even surrounding us. Flashes of heavy guns going off so close we got very excited, mainly we hoped to get some good food and cloths that there would a ceremony if we are liberated soon. But the floggings went on, after 25 lashes they were left in the Apel Platze center until of it they were able to drag themselves back to the barracks.

How many times over and over I wished in the this Buna Camp Auschwitz III that I could set my eyes and be able to see my strict father, especially our precious angelic mother, good brothers, and our only beautiful precious sister, and of course also our other many relatives tat we were close to so I could tell them that I really loved them and appreciated them being strict, correcting me, caring, and being close with me and for me.

My memory kept tricking me back to think and say "Dear God, if I could at least see, hear or touch them, how I would like to be asked by my parents, brothers, or other family members to let me do something for them, any chore, I certainly would not resent it." On the contrary, now I would appreciate if they would just ask me anything to do for them, I would do any chores and it would be a pleasure if given the chance. I would gladly do anything they would ask me seven times over. Unfortunately, now I am ordered by theses vicious fascists to do hard slave labor right or wrong to suit them immediately or die; in the least if my work did not please them, I would receive severe punishment if they thought that I did not obey.

Now that it is getting colder and am freezing in this miserable cold climate, I would very much appreciate y brothers' old clothing the hand-me-downs, but now I am forced to wear this stinky, thin striped torn uniform. At home we had plenty of water from the well, now I am given water to drink only when and if the guards deem it desirable for them not when we must have for our terrible undernourished thirsty body's needs. Unfortunately, I was not alone in this misery. Seeing others suffer all around me as I did made the hurt even worse, but somehow we just went on by setting our miseries aside and now, as the saying goes, we just kept rolling with the punches.

Standing at attention in the Apel Platze in line on our frozen feet sometimes for what seemed like hours, especially in the cold evening to be counted and hopefully get our meager ration of food was very difficult on us especially after a long grueling day of hard work, plus abuse, and the constant pain we endured from injuries we had no zest left. My frozen weak body ached as we stood in line hoping for some sustenance in the soup

Maybe the guy dishing out the soup ration with the ladle would dip down into the large pot and give me something solid from the bottom that contained a little nourishment, such as a piece of a potato or I would be one of the last ones for that pot to be lucky to get a larger piece of a potato or a maybe even sliver of meat. I craved for something of substance you always hoped to be the last one receiving soup from that pot, and of course the heavy bread not only contained sawdust but it felt and probably contained sand and mainly ground glass.

Here in this miserable camp, I matured very fast, especially for my young age and with my lack of education, I learned to appreciate life from the upbringing by my wonderful parents as well as learning from others. Refusing to give up I somehow continued to hope and pray that everyone in our family were alive, somewhere safe doing hopefully better than me, but most of all that they are not suffering like I and that somehow they are alive and well. I always remembered my promise to them that I would keep alive no mater what, so I had to keep trying harder and harder, so I could make it through each minute, hours, days, to endure the promise I made to my parents in the cattle car which took us to Auschwitz. I gave them my word of honor that no matter what I would try to survive. Maybe they wanted me to live so that I could make them proud of me surviving as well as tell the world what had happened to me to them and other decent people in what turned out to be the world's worst hell ever on earth, Auschwitz I, II, and here in Buna, Auschwitz III. We did not have any zest or joy left and we did not feel part of the human race.

Even before I was taken to the ghetto then shipped to Auschwitz I, II, and here in Auschwitz III, I came a long way into maturity and a little savvy or wisdom at a young age. I was

13 when I had to leave our home after the many fascist Hitler youth attacks upon us whilst still in our village and whenever I went or came home from school, then I went away from home first to one village then another village where we had family, then I ran away to Budapest, the capital of Hungary, after a while there I had to go back home because I was not allowed as a Jew that was not born there to stay in Budapest.

Because I learned as soon as I arrived in the camp to save my strength and my health as much as I could so I lived from minute to minute, hour to hour, and day to day. Here in Buna, I had to live with an animal instinct in order to survive the next moment. I tried hard never to call attention to myself especially in my weakened condition after all it was Germany's goal to eliminate us or at least take away our names, freedom our humanity and reduce us to senseless, nameless creatures, or disposing of us as a result we were to them vermin, our lives meant nothing to them.

Every day I longed for and kept my spirits up for a glimpse of the only brother, Sam, who was in this camp he was the only one I knew for sure that was still alive it gave me the extra courage I needed as a result I was able to pass many selections not to be picked for the gas chambers, I needed and I looked forward to seeing him and for him to stay alive because he was in the same camp. I knew absolutely about as a result was terribly worried also about the rest of our family; if they were alive or if so, where they might be.

When I was fortunate to see Sam, it was like looking at a messenger send by God. My love for him and the excitement that I felt when I could see him was like adrenalin into my veins. He was in a barrack at the other end of the camp, and even though we were close physically, it was forbidden to talk or socialize, even in the evening; being totally exhausted, so we could never really be with each other or spend any meaningful time together. There up to 60,000 people crammed into our tiny camp. The entire camp was maybe a few city blocks square, but it contained more people than most small cities that are several miles square. We were really crammed next to and on top of each other even in the bunks yet it felt that he was miles away.

I knew better than to publicly communicate or to be seen too much with Sam. I had to content myself just to see him alive on occasion. Not only both of us could be in trouble for socializing, but as punishment for such "crimes", our entire barracks could have their food withheld, and could have additional clean up detail assigned at night, mainly get beaten up or even worse.

I could not and would not bring that wrath on our fellow men as there was very little precious food or rest that was allotted to us. After all the Guards, Kapos, or Blockelsters were looking for excuses to punish us. We did not want to give them any more excuses or opportunities to vent their viciousness on us they took much of their anger and viciousness out on us without reason just to make our lives even more unbearable.

Even now, 50 years later, many horrible memories haunt me especially at night from this Buna camp, some memories are worse than others. I remember one day when they brought in a fresh bunch of healthy strong people from Alsace France, along with a new group of Jews from Hungary, Holland and other countries.

They were very healthy robust looking as most newcomers were several were assigned to our barrack and bunks. I shared a bunk with a celebrated Frenchman who vehemently denied being a Jew, or having any first or second generation Jewish ancestors. Another bunk mate was a famous Jewish physician from Germany who somehow managed for a few years to hide his Jewish identity and thereby avoid being arrested, and later a former Dutch aristocrat was put in a bunk above me. None of them professed to be Jewish in fact they were denying having any Jewish lineage.

Towards the middle of 1944, the SS were determined to cleanse Germany and all occupied European controlled countries of any vestige of Jews. To rid them of any vestige or lineage of Jews they began arresting anyone who had even the remotest trace of Jewish blood or connection, no matter how many generations ago. They also arrested anyone suspected of having shielded a Jew or if a Nazi hierarchy did not like someone they were arrested as Jews or cohorts, as a result they were deported and brought to Auschwitz the camps or other extermination camps. Some of them were then sent to Auschwitz III the camp of Buna where I was.

These aristocrats were used to luxurious homes, bed, furniture, the best of foods, formerly very in-group people they had a real shock when they were processed and given a skimpy stripped uniform very little food before they arrived to our camp. Soon upon there arrival, they were immediately assigned to do heavy manual labor just like the rest of us, they certainly did not expect this kind of heavy, physical abuse, or hard labor; and they certainly were not used to lack of food, as a result they could not cope with it to long.

Those of us who had been in this hellish place for awhile survived by shear guts and just because somehow or other we were able to ignore the hunger, pains, beatings, to go on blindly obeying orders, in fact, we were and acted like robots performing hard labor; most of the time, by the time the day was over; we did not have the strength to talk even among ourselves when we returned to our barracks from our long hard slave work day so we just laid down and collapsed in our bunks yet unable to sleep.

In spite of our emaciated condition, we did try to give courage to each other especially the new arrivals. Sometimes we had just a few minutes to whisper to each other before the lights went out if no guards, Blockelster or Kapo was around, or on the Apel Platze.

I seemed to have been one of the youngest and certainly the least educated in our bunk, barracks, or section. I don't know if it helped that I was young, naive and still lacking even a minimal elementary basic school education, I had very little common sense, etiquette, of general adult behavior or experience I am sure many felt sorry for me.

I felt very hollow among these educated, sophisticated aristocrats because even a proper elementary school education would have helped, and I certainly had no ability to communicate, especially in French, Dutch, Greek, Italian or some of the other languages these elite newcomers spoke. Even these well educated sophisticated, formerly wealthy or noble men were soon brought down to nothing; just like the rest of us they became weaklings, "musilman". Again it didn't matter what a person's stature in former life was; here he was just an undesirable person by the Nazis, he was just a Jew in this hellish place which they designed to dispose not only of us, but even any traces of us.

It was just a matter of time for them, just like for the rest of us, a day, a week, a month, or maybe three months here and they would be reduced in body and soul to a muselman, and they too would become nothing but skin and bones. All of us were to the Nazis just a number awaiting our demise. Everyone, no matter what their original status might have been, was soon reduced to a lifeless skinny body that would eventually be shipped back to Birkenau-Auschwitz I for gassing, if alive, and cremation, most of us knew it was just a matter of time but most of us refused to capitulate so we did not give in so easy we were determined to fight and retain our human traits in spite of the obstacles and dangers we faced.

I looked forward to my rare short conversations with these newcomers very quietly especially when the lights went out to interact with some of these fine, educated, sophisticated men. Somehow it made life a little more bearable in this hell hole. I respected their former status and splendor; above all they appeared to be nice. I felt sorry for them because they somehow tried to retain their good manners, but they could not maintain their facade for long, or handle it because they were brought down very low, like the rest of us to be; just an undesirable scum, "Jude" "Jew", condemned Jewish souls just like us. Most of the time they spoke to no one except maybe to me; for some reason they liked me and I was pleased because they were good people.

I was lucky that I understood several languages even at that young age, Czech, Hungarian, Polish, Ruskie, Yiddish and German. You could see in their eyes that they somehow trusted me. These people in our barracks especially one of them in the bunk next to me told me one night about the wonderful life that had been taken away from him how they had helped many of their Christian neighbors and friends who were high officials in the fascist German or Nazi government, and especially what they thought was their own kind, their former Christian friends and neighbors.

They were absolutely crushed because they found out that their grandparents left the Jewish faith, their parents were raised as Christians, and practiced Christianity. Those same fellow Christian friends, or even worse, that their Christian relatives had betrayed them. They were in terrible agony. Most of the time they were crying with their heart and eyes open, they seeming to hear and see nothing of the horrible reality going on around them. There was something very pathetic in their muteness.

Not too long ago, maybe a couple of weeks or a month ago they were successful respected Christian people, doctors, professors, businessmen, engineers, or even Nazi officials or fascists. Now in this place they were not even part of everyday ordinary human beings; they certainly could not be eating or enjoying what they used to eat so in a very short time they started to become weaklings, "muselman," like the rest of us.

Even though I became friends with them and they rarely talked when they could about themselves, their families or the circumstances which brought them to this hell called Auschwitz III, Buna, they just could not cope with the harshness of the reality here. Suddenly finding themselves in such a pitiful sub existence, the kind of or even worse lack of food, if you want to call it that, which was less than bare sustenance and being treated worse than animals like the rest of us they had completely and quickly been taken from their old gracious lives which had been not to long ago full of happiness, laughter, camaraderie, drinking, eating whenever and whatever they desired, probably getting along with the Nazi hierarchy, their successes in the business, community, medicine, charitable involvements, most of all their former fascist or Nazi involvement or association gave them what they thought security now they lost it just like the rest of us Jews.

All the joys that Hitler and the fascists' actions had surrounded them with and their families before they were brought here, and now it was suddenly gone. Now they were just a number condemned just like the rest of us, probably full of lice just like us, forced to march to cadence back and forth, to and from work, perform unbelievable hard slave labor, or to stand in the cold in our weak starving condition for some meager food or to be at attention freezing to be counted on the Apel Platze, before we were allowed to go back into the barracks.

When we lay down on the rough wooden board bunks, we muttered to ourselves and talked to ourselves reminiscently about our families and loved ones, and most of all, the decent lives that we lost and really appreciated now the thing we had not too long ago that were taken from us, for me it seemed many centuries ago. A lot of us were hoping, fearfully but in reality, not really expecting to see our loved ones again, especially the very young, older or weaker people who were by now probably crippled enough or be disposed of by our task masters.

We felt that even if we were not killed any time immediately, they were using some of us for medical experiments. There was no way to avoid the suffering and be all right again; in addition to all the "tzores" (problems) we were exposed to.

Yet most of us refused to abandon hope of someday soon being freed and be reunited with our loved ones. This was probably the most painful of all our suffering; not knowing, seeing, or hearing about your loved ones, but somehow we just kept holding on to our fragile life and hope they are alive and OK.

Most of us had relatives in England, Israel, formerly Palestine, or the "Golden Medina," the golden country of America, and we knew that if we didn't make it through these camps at least some of our relatives would survive. Even in our despicable existence, it was not cowardice to believe the impossible that some of us Jews would survive somewhere on the face of this earth.

Prior to those days especially when a Jewish boy was born in Europe or America, his parents believe and hoped that he will become a success as a professional, a Tailor, Rabbi, scholar, tradesman, businessman or maybe a doctor, but in Germany or France that he will enter the institute of higher learning, to become a professor or in England that they hoped he would be a great success or would be knighted.

To most of us in the old backward part of the European country, especially in the Carpathian Mountains, the Jews were taught to be very religious and hopefully to become a rabbi, tailor, shoe maker, baker or a Hebrew teacher.

Even now under these horrid sufferings I remembered learning in Hebrew school, that our Bible teaches us that nothing seems impossible if you study your Bible, keep the Sabbath Holy, follow the commandments, believe in God and yourself, after all, the only thing left for us here in Buna was a very remote hope of survival. If you gave that up, you were a goner. We prayed and hoped that soon, very soon justice would triumph over evil. Above all, it seemed to us a given even would occur for the miraculous deliverance of our people to freedom, and we were hoping and praying that Germany and its fascist allies would soon lose the war, that the allies would be victorious, without any more casualties and we would regain our freedom again live as normal healthy free working respectable people. Even in the darkest times, our dreams and hopes kept us going, praying for redemption, a decent future; plenty of good food, good health, and these feelings of hope somehow kept us alive.

Things did not get easier for us even though it was obvious the Nazis were suffering losses on many fronts, especially in the Russian front, however they did not let up on us; our suffering and slave work kept going on and on. The allies, mostly British military planes, were seen by us bombing the factory we were working in Buna III, the I.G. Industrial complex they were targeting the industrial complex first every week, then every second or third day. Then it was every day, one time a bomb fell real close to us it knocked me down and some of the bombs hit the building we were working in, setting it on fire and of course, we had to clear up the rubble from the bombs, repair the damage to the buildings, roads, repair railroad tracks, and do the other repairs after each allied bomb attacks. Unfortunately many of our people were killed by bombs, the shrapnel were flying all around us or some of our people were buried under the dirt. We were envious of those that were killed, because they will not have to suffer anymore.

The rumors kept floating that we would be liberated soon by the victorious Allies. The Red army was just around the corner we heard explosions not to far away. Fascism would be banished from the face of the earth forever and all Fascists, SS, Gestapo and Einzatz Groupen and their collaborators will be caught arrested and sentenced for their vicious criminal acts against us Jews and others.

Finally the Germans had us start loading up the large trucks and to fill the railroad cars to the maximum capacity we were forced to work night and day, especially loading the sophisticated equipment that was stored in the warehouses where we worked obviously they wanted the valuables to be shipped out away from Poland and the Russians, into the interior of Germany the SS somehow were still sure the fascists will prevail in dominating the world for a thousand years, what they called their thousand year Reich.

As time went on, we were expecting the British or other bombers to target the factory and warehouses constantly, but they only came once or twice a day and we also prayed that they would bomb the rail road tracks leading to the death factory camps especially to Birkenau-Auschwitz I to stop the killings of our people. Sometimes the bombers even skipped several days. We heard the sirens then we saw the planes dropping bombs, sometimes in frustration and in our emancipated condition, we were hoping that one of the bombs would fall on top of us and take us out of our misery, or bomb our camp, especially the watch towers and electrified fences, so maybe some of us could escape, but no such luck they did not bomb our camp.

After we emptied most of the equipment, machinery, and other items from the factories and storage buildings onto the many rail road cars and large trucks, there was no doubt that these loaded trains were taken back as quickly as possible under darkness to the interior of Germany because our camp was located near Krakow and Auschwitz in occupied Poland getting closer and closer to the Russian front the Germans fiercely feared revenge from the Russian soldiers because of what they probably did to them.

Unfortunately, we did not realize it, but after we emptied and loaded all the merchandise, we were next on the list of items to be moved, or evacuated. We were kind of hoping, praying and wishing the SS Guards would be forced to flee and abandon us so we would finally be liberated by the allies, we didn't care, probably even if we were liberated by the Russians, so that we might have a chance to feel human again hopefully to have a decent meal, some decent clothing, a real bed to sleep in, and a home or decent shelter. But the SS would not let us alone for even a moment, certainly not to be able to stay, escape or survive here.

I cannot help but recall one time after a bombing attack when we were clearing the rubble away from the fire inside the warehouse we worked in, and as we hacked away at the rubble we realized there was a big unexploded bomb. We were ordered to clear the rubble around it, then we had to tie ropes around it and pull it out slowly by hand from the building, as we lowered the unexploded bomb into a hole or crater where another bomb fell only a few hours ago, just then the bomb which was set with a timer went off killing several of our comrades. Had it exploded one second earlier I also would have been a goner with them.

Many times during the bombing, pieces of shrapnel from the bombs were flying in all directions around us, but as soon as the bombers left the area, the SS emerged screaming and ordering us to work faster and faster, repairing the damaged rail road tracks, the roads, and other things, such as a building. However, when darkness fell, we were marched back to camp as usual after 16 hours or more of grueling work to dismantle the factory everything they could was loaded on the RR freight cars or trucks destined for the interior of Germany. We noticed the SS celebrating the arrival of the New Year 1945 but gloomily.

When we arrived back at the camp late that evening a group of young SS men came by again with specially trained German shepherd dogs which were trained to attack our vitals. We were not strong enough to fight them off. Finally one of the SS men called them off before they got to me. Yes we feared the folks Deutsche, the real Germans, but we were even more scared of the collaborators, Russian, Cossack, Polish, Lithuanians, and Ukraine Fascist who joined the elite SS guards mostly because they seemed to revel in making us suffer and they did not want us alive to tell about them when and if the Russians arrived to liberate us.

The more we suffered the more they seemed to enjoy it. Even now, they took pleasure in probing us with their bayonets, kicking us in our ankles and legs with their heavy boots. Their legs were strong and healthy and when they kicked us, they could easily break our weak bones. The Ukrainian fascists also used every excuse to whip us, they were vicious beyond human comprehension, especially when we were unable to lift or move very heavy items; things that would have been difficult to move for big strong healthy people, we had to do it fast in our very weak condition or they would whip us. I remember one of the many times the Ukrainian SS guards would take great delight in using their boots to kick us, their whips to whip us, or the rifle butts to hit us just to bring us pain. One big heavy Ukrainian stepped on friend's head after he knocked him down and crushed the skull of the boy who used to lie next to me in the bunk. Unfortunately, the person lasted only a couple of days after such abuse. Then I watched with sorrow as he was thrown onto the pile with the other dead bodies to be shipped for cremation to Auschwitz.

Unfortunately, this type of punishment was meted out to us frequently, especially as the German Army started suffering defeat on most fronts, but especially the Russian front as the Nazis were scared of them more than the others because they no doubt performed many atrocities against Russians or their soil which they occupied.

Not all barracks or work details experienced the exact same abuses, for some reason the SS men were always coming up with new and improved ways to torture our section. We were not supposed to last long anyway and they felt it was their job to see to it that we did not last longer than was absolutely necessary, but somehow some of us were still managing to hold on, to stay alive; our camp and barrack was filled constantly to capacity with the new people who were brought in almost to the last days.

The eight miserable months I spent in Buna Auschwitz III, seemed like eight horrible unbelievable, miserable lifetimes, certainly the kind of abuse, hunger and other sufferings we were forced to endure are not experienced by humans anywhere, and I hope they never will be.

As soon as we arrived this one day back to the camp in late afternoon when we got back into the barrack trying to unwind from the hard work there came this horrible creepy scream "Rouse" "out" from the Blockelster, who ordered us to assemble on the Apel Platze again to be checked out by our tattoos on our left arm. This would show who was still alive.

This evening it seemed something wasn't going right for the SS, as they seemed in a panicky mood, yet still very cocky and in control. Suddenly the order was given again to start marching this time out of the camp, certainly not to work this late in the I.G. Farben Industry. I had a scary feeling we found out later that it was January 17, 1945 that I had bid goodbye Buna, Auschwitz III. Little did we realize that we were heading for the kind of death march that most of us were not to survive. Most of us new we were in terrible physical and emotional shape, yet refusing to realize just what bad shape we were really in. Now we were lined up again in ranks of five with guards on both sides, the cadence started "Eins, Zwei, Drei, again!" as we were forced to move quickly and to leave this camp for a destination or purpose unknown to any of us and from which most of us would not survive. It was getting dark and very bitterly cold this time of the year. The snow was falling hard with a lashing wind but I had no choice but to walk straight head up just keep moving even though I had no strength left they marched us if we slow down or we try to escape we will be shot on the spot then they gave us orders to move out forward march. To this day, I can still close my eyes and smell the horrible odors we lived with day in and day out; they are forever embedded in my memory bank. Will that SS man's screams ever stop eating away at me? Will I or can I ever forget or set the sufferings I endured in this camp aside? I can only pray that someday, somehow, I will be able to cleanse or live with those sufferings that I had lived with and endured, day in and day out for so long.

I see it all these horrors over and over from my memory. I try not to think of bad things but these horrors keep coming back again and again. Yet I know that I need to remember in order to pass these horrible unbelievable memories of my experiences on to future generations to make sure other humans will not be subjected to or will never permit such inhumane acts or treatment by fellow man against any humans no matter what religion, faith, nationality, color, where they are from or who they are, no matter what excuse, motive, or reason they use people must treat each other humanly. I wanted to leave misery, horrors, and suffering behind me and start feeling human and free again.

Even after I was liberated I could not sleep at night for a long time certainly not more than two or three hours a night if I was lucky. Staying awake brought back some of those horrid pains from this and other camps when we did not have any mattress, straw to cushion the sores on our aching bodies or a blanket to keep us warm in the bitter cold or to cushion the hard rough wooden boards and the small space in which we had to try to sleep on empty starved stomachs. Now it seems very difficult even for me to believe that it was not a nightmare but real hell on earth that it was indeed real suffering I was forced to endure and yet be able to survive.

The camps demonstrated many things about inhumanity of man against man. It is proof that unfortunately humans are capable of committing the most heinous worst kind of evil acts that are conceived. All these vicious crimes and atrocities have been committed by normal fellow humans.

It is also proof that apathetic none caring people are just as responsible and guilty as those who actually performed these criminal acts. There was plenty of time they could have stopped it but they chose to ignore it which is one of the main reasons Hitler and his cohorts were encouraged and succeeded to precede post haste with their criminal actions.

Chapter 5: The Ride from Gleiwitz to Buchenwald

After the unbelievable forced march from Buna to Gleiwitz, when most of our people did not make it, it is still difficult for me even after fifty years, to try to remember something so horrific, let alone the exact details to be able to relate about that event, the horrible cold that year as we were being shoved into open coal carrying rail cars for the ride from Gleiwitz to Buchenwald, which took five or seven days, whilst it occurred so many years ago. Even for me it is very difficult to believe that I survived such misery and suffering which was beyond human endurance. All of these years I wanted and, indeed, did block it out of my mind and hoped that maybe it had never happened to me. That it was just a bad nightmare. This trip was certainly one of those horrific sufferings which are beyond human comprehension or belief. I still have great difficulty believing that it happened to me, even though I was one of the few that survived it, now I must be recalling or talking about it, because it was so unbelievable. I was cold and in terrible pain from hunger and thirst that a normal mind cannot fathom the suffering we endured on that trip, let alone believe that it actually occurred to me and many others and still be able to survive.

We were all "Muselmen" emaciated, scrounge, ready to die, but we were forced to move, screamed and cussed at (schnell Yude) "quick Jew", as we were being hurriedly loaded for departing the area of Gleiwitz, Poland, one of the Auschwitz concentration camps after what I can only describe as the most unbelievable death march we had from Buna Auschwitz III, to get here. We were in Gleiwitz only a short time, a day or so, they gathered our few surviving people "Katzetniks" camp prisoners, here from most of the Auschwitz sub-camps for shipment to the interior of Germany, I guess they needed cheap slave labor. We were terribly confused, tired, very weak, and bewildered (to say the least), and if that was not enough, the short tempered guards again began to scream at us, (Yude. raus, Schnell) "Jew out fast", cuss at us to shove us into the waiting coal carrying topless railroad box cars in the worst part of winter. I was again separated form my only brother Sam, again I was fortunate enough to see him still alive in Gleiwitz even if he was very weak and it was only for a short time, but at least I saw him alive.

The separation this time from Sam was even more difficult and painful for me to cope with than before, because this time I thought for sure I would never see him again, especially in our weakened, emaciated conditions and the vicious way the guards treated us on the death march from Buna to Gleiwitz and now in this miserable cold, to shove us in to the open coal carrying cars without a cover or heat was scary.

How can I or anyone of us ever forget this miserable train ride in the icy cold weather in a steel bottom and sides coal car? There was no roof on the cars to protect us day or night from the miserable cold winter and fierce wind. We were still in the Polish Szylasian Mountains which are known for bad, fierce, cold winter weather, and we are again exposed to the howling, icy cold windy weather which blew cold air and snow all around and through us with nothing to protect us. As I remember it, during the day it was bad enough, but at night, the temperature must have been 20 to 30 degrees below zero. We were totally unprepared, especially in our emaciated rundown, starved condition, and totally unprotected in our thin torn striped uniforms, without even underwear, socks, a roof or blanket over our heads.

Each and every one of us were in agony as we were exposed to the cruel ice cold, surrounded with metal on the sides and the bottom, without a top or anything to protect us. There is no doubt we were truly treated like lifeless coal and not people. We were still very close to Auschwitz where they burned our people; coal probably was brought with these RR cars to burn us humans.

Many Polish civilians looked at us, but did nothing to help us. We were pleading for food and water or snow but not one of them lifted a finger to help us in our misery. We were wedged into each of these small coal carrying cars large enough to accommodate maybe 30 to 40 men; but they managed to shove in 100 to 120 of us into such cars. As it was, we were barely alive; trying to hang on to what ever life was left in us. I felt like a sardine squeezed into a topless square tin can, crammed in so tight that it caused pain because I had sores all over my body, especially on my feet from the non stop three or four day forced march. There was no moving around, certainly no room to sit or lay down to rest our weary bodies, but the worst pain to me was I had nothing to eat, drink, or cover my face and open sores from the continuous penetrating, howling, freezing wind and snow. We stood like wooden soldiers crumpled but somehow clinging to life (with varying degrees of success) only after several hours of not moving were we finally starting to take off. Meanwhile, we just stood there freezing. Somehow we did not expect them to and surely they did not feed us or give us water or warm clothes to keep us warm. We tried to cuddle, hug or rub against each other. Even having gone without sex for a long time, none of the men even thought about it or made any advances, the entire time in the camps and certainly not here.

Finally, the coal cars loaded with us, their human cargo, started to move. At first the cars were jerked back and forth until they put us on the right track late in the darkness. We were very hungry and cold also terribly thirsty. The train finally started to move forward, at first chugging along ever so slowly, then sometimes at speeds of up to 50 miles an hour with a 20 to 30 mile an hour blistering icy wind blowing in our faces. It was here that I experienced the most excruciating pain a human can ever experience or withstand. It was what appeared to be the longest, hungriest, coldest, thirstiest cooped up ride of human suffering ever without food or even worse, without water. The worst part of the train ride apart from the hunger and cold, beyond a shadow of a doubt, was the suffering of excruciating thirst pain, which I learned, to my dismay, is more painful than anything or any pain I ever experienced before or since.

Especially as we passed or sometimes stopped at railroad stations or under bridges with roads overhead, we might be lucky to have a piece of sleet or ice from above, fall on us. If it did, the ice was literally like "Manna" from Heaven. The icicle at that time tasted better than any chocolate or dessert that I have ever tasted before or since. Many of our people were too weak or could not free their hands to catch the precious ice or snow flakes, when it came down, our manna from heaven. Some of my comrades would bite their desperate lips or arms to try to make them bleed so hopefully they could get moisture on their lips and in their mouths. Unfortunately, most of us had very little blood or strength left in our bodies. No doubt this insatiable thirst pain was the worst pain I ever experienced. It was so painful; it was beyond being unbearable that I saw someone somehow muster up enough strength to tear his own guts out with his own fingers, because he could not tolerate this horrific pain from the thirst any more.

What made it even worse and more painful was seeing the uncaring German or Polish civilians looking at us, watching us many times at railroad stations, or when we were stopped under bridges. We were heartsick, amazed and dumbfounded to see sometimes hundreds of people, many women and children, were just standing and nonchalantly watching us begging them for snow, ice, food, above all water, or any help. One time, it had to be a Sunday, because they were dressed that way, when mothers and children were coming from church, I saw them holding Bibles, they just looked at us freezing, starving emaciated people without any caring or human emotions. How could they look into our eyes and see us half dead people in the coal cars without caring or with no human reaction? They certainly were not thinking or trying to help their fellow humans. How could they stand on the bridges, or at the railroad station just looking at us without any human emotions, not giving a damn; surely Hitler and Fascism did not eliminate totally their human instincts and replace it with uncaring hate. I just could not comprehend what kind of family they are bringing up. Will they or could their children ever be decent humans?

Many times when our train stopped, we pleaded with onlookers to please help us with food or water. We even pleaded for them to throw us a snowball or and icicle, unfortunately to no avail. Even though we stood sometimes for hours in one place, we saw them feeding children or eating, it seemed they had plenty of food or time to get us some food at least a little ice, a snowball, or water. Some of them had baskets of food. They saw us helpless, almost dead, humans but did not care for us one iota. It seemed to us that there was no humane thinking, caring, or people anywhere at that time, especially in Germany or Nazi Poland caring or trying to help fellow humans. It was very emotionally and physically painful for us to see the people just nonchalantly watching us dying as we were pleading to them for help, especially as they were eating sandwiches, fruit or desserts, of course they were dressed warm, while looking at us, they saw we were dying from starvation or freezing to death from the bitter cold, in our thin uniform without even underwear or socks, and suffering terribly from thirst. Some of them even pointed at us and drew the attention of others, especially the children at our misery, probably making comments, "they are Jews".

If they would have had any compassion or human traits in them they could have thrown us some desperately needed food, even just a crumb, or at least some snow, water or an old blanker, or some old clothes, but clearly they chose not to care or to do anything to help us in our misery. After all, we were just Jews in their prison stripped uniforms, condemned to be eliminated from the face of this earth. I cannot believe how they looked and stared at us as though we did not exist. This inhumane, painful experience; to me proves beyond any doubt, how people could become uncaring it was for me, very torturous and still is beyond comprehension.

There were all kinds of nationalities that did not act human, not just Germans but Polish, Lithuanians, Ukrainian, Hungarian and others; how could they be so cruel to us fellow humans? Did Fascism and Hitler take all their human traits or feelings away from them? Did they totally lose their conscience and human hearts? They saw us almost dead humans (muselman) with our pleading outstretched arms, begging for a little food and water or a little ice or snow; but each and every one of them ignored or pretended they did not see or hear us plead with them. No wonder we felt totally abandoned by the world because there was no emotion whatsoever from them or others, there absolutely no concern for us their fellow humans.

Even though the journey might have taken only four to seven days, because we were so week, starved, terribly cold and so very thirsty; time stood still; the pain was eating away at us, each minute seemed like a day, each hour like a month, and each day like an eternity. Many people in our coal car with their frail starved bodies were momentarily near death or too weak to keep on fighting to keep alive so they succumbed to the bitter cold, other pains or the hunger and above all, the terrible thirst pain. A lot of our people died within the first or second day in this death ride, and unfortunately we could not help them. Those of us that had a little energy left, including me, crawled under the dead frozen bodies to protect ourselves from the howling winds and the bitter cold. At least for a little while their bodies retained some warmth and weren't completely ice cold and stiff. After awhile the bodies smelled awful and turned into a motionless clump of ice.

We were transported and passed through many towns and villages, stopping often for switching or passing trains in both directions. There were also quite a few air raid sirens in action, especially when the train stopped completely with allied attack planes overhead. After a few days in that cold steel (coal carrying) car without toilets; (even though the dead bodies were frozen) the stench in the railroad cars became unbearable. Those of us that somehow managed to stay alive got rid of, or lost our bodily fluids and excrement standing up in our clothing, and this would freeze on our scant clothing and bodies. We were still wearing only the same thin badly torn striped uniforms that were issued to us almost a year ago upon our arrival in Auschwitz I. Some of us managed to take off some of the clothes from the dead inmates' bodies and put it on ourselves before the bodies froze as solid as ice. Our clothes were pretty well worn and rotten from the filth, mud, dirt, urine, sweat, even blood and every kind of excrement the body can produce so an extra jacket, pants or two helped a lot, (I even got a pair of regular shoes from a dead body that were a few sizes too large for me) so I discarded my wooden clogs, it too helped a little in this unbearable chill. And every time the train stopped or started to move it jerked, making us fall amongst or on top of the frozen dead bodies which by now stunk to high heaven and were as hard as ice causing more pain on our bodies that were full of sores when we fell on them.

Unfortunately, the frozen dead bodies could not completely keep the howling wind and cold off of us indefinitely. Only a few of us in the car somehow managed to live through this unbelievably nightmarish experience; mainly because we were determined to hold onto our fragile lives no matter what suffering we endured, I felt somehow some of us had to survive.

Only God knows the reason why or how some of us survived, probably some of us, I am sure, were determined to be witness to the horrors that we endured at the hand of these former so-called humans who became fascist, then sadistic killing monsters. Some of us lived with the hope that maybe soon we would be liberated and reunited with members of our family. I remembered the commitment to our parents to survive. I still harbored hope that our beloved parents and our other brothers, sister, uncles, aunts, cousins were alive.

Obviously we had no idea where we were headed nor what was in store for us after such a tortuous, chilling ride that took four to seven days and lasted what seemed a hellish eternity for us. The final destination, we found out when we arrived and the train stopped, that it was a camp called Buchenwald. I remember once at one of our stops overhearing the guards walking around the train making sure none of us could escape, talking amongst themselves just before we arrived, that we were headed there. They boasted that if any of us arrived alive, which they doubted, that this was the last stop for us Jews on our life's journey.

The train finally arrived at Camp Buchenwald near Weimar, and stopped inside the electrified, heavily guarded camp. When the locks from the steel door were opened from the outside, the guard's orders again were screamed at us. "Schnell" "Raus" to get out fast from the car. "Raus Yude! Out Jew!" but unfortunately most of the people in ours as well as the other cars were dead. Out of approximately one hundred to one hundred twenty people in the coal car I was in, who began this hellish journey from the Gleiwitz camp with me, only eight of us barely got off alive. The others were dead, by then stiff, frozen bodies.

Again we stared at tall electrified barbed wire fences with watch towers surrounding the camp and an iron sign at the entrance into the camp was similar to the one that so called were welcoming us to Auschwitz, "Arbeit Macht Frei", (Work Makes Free). Since we were too weak, they brought other inmates to remove the hundreds, if not thousands of dead comrades' bodies to be burned in the crematorium or were mass buried in large pits in the adjoining forest.

Once those of us who were alive were assembled in the center of the Buchenwald camp, we were checked out and registered by our tattoo numbers. We were marched to the interior of the camp, away from the Apel Platze. Again, we could smell the awful stench form the crematoria. It was the same horrible stench I remembered from the Auschwitz I Birkenau ovens; burning human flesh. We soon realized that we were on another unholy ground. After the roll call, we were given two slices of real bread; we were counted again and marched of to the assigned barracks.

We heard cries not only from our group, but also from the previous arrivals. People were dying a miserable death from the same or similar torturous trip as we had just endured in the open coal carrying railway cars. We were fortunate that once we got inside the Buchenwald camp, close to the "apel platze", they gave us a ladle of warm soup, it tasted fantastic. We gulped it down immediately, and miracle of miracle they also gave us again two slices of real bread. I cried, kissed and licked that precious bread. It tasted better than any candy or dessert, or any treat that I have had before or since. I looked up to heaven to thank the Almighty. As we were being counted and checked out again by our tattoo we were assigned to a barrack, and because of our pitiful condition we had some how a little time to rest before being harassed in a few days or worked again to death. After a few days, I got a little stronger because we got food two or three times a day. I started to look for my brothers, especially Sam, amongst the other recent arrivals. I was so scared because I could not find him at first. I felt a great petrifying fear that I would never find him or see him again. The fears made me shake. Similar fears came from the very few others of us surviving souls as to what had happened to our families that had been brought to Auschwitz with us. We got some food and water again in the evenings, which perked us up even though we were inside the gates of our new hell on earth called Buchenwald.

I am sure I won't, but if I live to be several hundred years I shall never be able to comprehend the uncaring, inaction of the German civilians, as well as the Austrian, Polish, Ukrainian, and hundreds of other people, especially the women and young people that saw us pleading, as we were near death, for food or water. Some of them even laughed and none would reach out a helping hand to a fellow human.

Even now 50 years later, when I see a coal carrying car I can't help but feel the pain and suffering I endured on that trip, it especially reminds me of that time I am still seeing my fellow man totally uncaring about our sufferings. I am also reminded of many of my fellow sufferers freezing to death, or of me standing up or hiding under the frozen dead bodies to protect myself from the killer cold wind and ice. Most of all, I cannot forget how we suffered excruciating pain form lack of water, even though we pleaded with them, the people did not even throw us an icicle or snow ball. This was beyond any doubt the longest and most painful vicious days of suffering, I or any human has ever endured or experienced.

The memory of my suffering as well as the horrific looks and unbelievable suffering of my follow man in that coal carrying cold car will no doubt torment me the rest of my life, especially pleading with them, holding onto them, trying to keep them alive and being uncaringly surrounded by so many civilian men, women children of my fellow humans. Even friends did not care about our unbelievable sufferings and finally the death because most ordinary people were apathetic, but most were hateful fascist monsters or just did not care about their fellow man. I hope that from now on the world will never permit the kind of sufferings on any humans or animals that we were forced to endure on that trip.

How did I survive? Only God knows. No doubt with His help and the help and support of friends, kind deeds from fellow sufferers and determination. Perhaps because of my promise to father and mother that no matter what, I must survive. We tried to restrain our human traits, in spite of the dangers, obstacles, sufferings and out last the hate mongers. The people of Germany created Auschwitz and the killing centers because they were determined to rule the world by hate, terror and murders. Auschwitz and this trip was absolute evil, a warning of what mankind is capable of.

Chapter 6: Trip to, and Arrival in, New York

Finally the time came for me to depart from my temporary but trustful home in Britain, which was almost like a rebirth and partial recovery from the camp sufferings. The time had arrived to leave this temporary place. Because of our wonderful Uncles and Aunts who came in the 1900s to America and had sent us papers so we could immigrate to America, after several years' effort, I, along with my brothers and sister were fortunate enough to be able to go to America and rejoin most of my surviving family and the rest of my American relatives.

All of us orphaned children who lost their parents in the Holocaust, that were brought by British Jews to England after WWII, especially those of us who were able to immigrate to America were excited and upbeat as some of us left London for the Liverpool, England docks to board a ship for the ultimate trip to the "Golden Medina," America. For me it was truly fulfilling our life long dreams of finally being united with my only surviving Aunts, Uncles and their families and of course with that we kindled our hopes for a decent life and more solid future.

I could not help but think in remorse a great deal as we were on our way to the docks, especially of my beloved parents as well as so many relatives who were killed in Auschwitz along with all of our other elders. Unfortunately we lost most of our family, including almost all my cousins, in Europe. Thank God my five brothers, my sister and I miraculously survived. Now I am very upbeat heading for the dream land of America, where we had our only living Aunts and Uncles.

My brothers, who got there from Czechoslovakia about a year ago, and our sister that was with me, arrived in America from Britain a year earlier. Unfortunately our oldest brother, Fillip and his family were still trapped in the Soviet Union and our brother Sam who was still trying to recover from injuries that he suffered in the way of liberation for the state of Israel.

Just to arrive at the embarkation docks in Liverpool and looking at that beautiful huge ship called The Queen Mary, on which we were to travel, was breathtaking. It was a glorious, beautiful day as we were boarding the huge, elegant ship. To me it was a breathtaking, marvelous day, even though it was very chilly that morning and I was leaving my wonderful adopted caring Ralph family in Croydon, England. I loved them and was very much appreciative of their kindness and generosity to Sam, Rosalyn and me. It was also difficult leaving many of my friends with whom we developed a fantastic camaraderie. I had become very close to most of the boys and girls from the various orphanages, especially in London, as well as my friends that were working in the George Nissel Contact Lens Company and of course the social Primrose Club which was formed specially for us orphaned, children survivors of the Holocaust to help us recover mentally, physically and socially.

I was very much looking forward to having my life-long dream become reality. I wanted to go to America since I was a very young boy, especially when I got to know this cute girl from Chicago, Illinois; Janet Weiss, a visitor to our village, from America. She along with our elders told me so much about the Golden Land she called America. I fell in love then with America and Janet at that tender age of 8 or 9, when she and her mother visited their family who lived across from us. During their visit Janet and I were inseparable. I had never experienced such luxury or a great feeling before. They hired a chauffeur-driven limousine, which was almost unheard of in our area. In fact, there were very few automobiles to be seen in our part of Europe especially in our village back in those days, most of our roads were not even paved, even today, as we saw when we visited it fifty years later. The entire time she was there we were constantly on the move going swimming in the nearby Latorca River, which bordered our village, and on picnics on the side of the man-made bastion. We ate real American candy that they brought with them and I could get as much of it as I wanted, along with the fine grapes grown here and they could afford eating at the most desirable places in the adjoining city of Mukachevo.

Of course it helped that I was named Jacob (Yankele) after Janet's grandfather who was our neighbor and friend from across the street. They owned the bakery where Mother baked her bread, which was probably the reason to begin with that I was treated as "family" by them. Everyone in our village felt that this Weiss family from America were real millionaires, and of course that in America everybody was rich, all of us felt it was truly a country of haven, filled with golden opportunities. I recalled that it was my fondest wish, hope, and dream ever since then to be reunited with her, even during horrific sufferings and incarceration in the extermination camp I was thinking and dreaming of her. I was hoping beyond hope to survive the camps then hopefully go to America so I could be reunited with my Janet and or course our American family the wonderful Uncles and Aunts who sent packages, our parents always talked about them gleefully.

I enjoyed very much the Weiss family warmth, friendship, and the time I spent with these visitors, it made me want even more to immigrate to America and start my life anew so that I too could live in a healthy, decent environment which unfortunately was unable to achieve in our smell village of Palanok or anywhere else in Europe so far. I knew and have had the confidence in myself that if I worked hard and used my head to do the right things I should be able to accomplish some success if I have the opportunity to use the very best of my ability in America.

When we arrived at the docking yard in Liverpool for the purpose of leaving England, there was no doubt I was really ready for my new life in America and very much upbeat, I had on brand new tailored suit from Lord and Taylors, I even had on new shoes which Mom Ralph bought for me. Several of my friends from the orphanages who also belonged to the Primrose Club with me, boarded the luxury liner, "Queen Mary," with me heading for America to meet their only family left alive. We were very excited and could hardly wait to be going to the Golden Land. I wanted to be reunited with our brothers, sister, meet and get to know the Aunts and Uncles, our American families, and most of all to have a chance for a decent life and for our dreams to be reunited with the surviving family finally to come true. We boarded quickly, even though I was sad to leave the Ralph family but very excited for what was ahead of me. The ship's whistle for take off sounded and soon we really took off, we all felt that our life was going to be started anew as the beautiful ship passed through the slips and out into the December rainy, windy, cold rough Atlantic Ocean. When we left the harbor of Liverpool I was so excited that I could hardly eat the fine food that was served to us in the huge, stately, luxurious Queen Mary dining room. Obviously I felt this beautiful dining room was designed and furnished for royalty and wealthy people, not young paupers like my orphan friends and myself. Naturally, we were all overly exuberant to think like normal people or to really be able to appreciate its stately beauty.

Of course, we traveled and bought tickets the cheapest way possible, third, fourth or tourist class. I was in a room on the lowest deck with double bunks above and beside of me which accommodated four of us in small rooms of this magnificent ship. This lowest portion of the ship was not redone yet, since it was used to transport troops during WWII. Yet we were so upbeat, that we felt as if we were traveling to heaven in first class. We sang happy songs in Yiddish, Polish, Czech, Hungarian, and especially after each of our scrumptious evening dinners we sure ate a lot to make up for the years of lack of food. After we went dancing which I loved and enjoyed very much some of us were good enough to enter the dance contests which combined all class travelers. I was lucky and won one of the ballroom final dance contests, so I was asked to dance with several good dancers, some were real lovely ladies. I was fortunate to have met some of the loveliest American girls. They were flirtatious, some were married, as well as single girls of all ages, and were all traveling on the ship first and second or third class. It came natural so we flirted with each other. They let down their hair to entice us to dance with them and of course we were never exposed to such luxury and graciousness so we took the bait. I danced with them all night; it was all great fun. I have special fond memories of those events to this day especially about some of the lovely women, the flirting and dancing on this wonderful journey to haven my future home called America. I became friends with some very nice people from many different parts of America who tried to stay in touch with me for awhile. But I had no money, even to return the long distance phone calls and did not know how to write in English, or what I could write. I could tell them I got a job in a knitting mill in Ellwood City, PA, earning a measly $18.00 a week which to me was a lot but peanuts to them? Or how tough it is to get started in a new country without money amongst new people with strange customs or the problem I had with the new language dialogue, then getting a job in my trained profession, but nothing really changed my feeling, I was very upbeat about the American way of life and its opportunities. I had confidence in myself, my American family, but above all, I had faith in the American system and its people, after all the millions of poor uneducated people that came here from all parts of the world where they struggled for a chance to succeed but did not make it, now here in America most of them that worked hard did succeed some beyond their wildest dreams.

Most of my survivor friends that stayed in England, who were orphans with me had no relatives alive in Europe or America because their parents and all their other family members were murdered by the Nazis in the killing centers of Europe. As a result, some of our boys and girls stayed in Great Britain or went to Israel, like our brother, Sam who volunteered and went to fight for Israel to have a country of our own, to make sure there will be a Jewish State where we could be safe and make sure that statehood would become a reality that if we had to go someplace, we would have a place that would welcome us.

Those of us, who had living relatives that immigrated in the 1920 to America, wanted to immigrate to America, just like me or were traveling to meet their American families for the first time. For us the Americans were the only surviving living elders, I considered them patriarchs of our family. Our Aunts and Uncles that were alive came before the war to the United States. Most of my friends on the boat had no one, no brothers or sisters left that survived in Europe after the Holocaust, the few lucky ones only had an Uncle or Aunt alive that had come to America in the 1920's. I was lucky. I had five brothers and one sister who survived the Holocaust. Most of us except Philip and Sam sailed to America with no grandiose ideas or false illusions of money growing on trees or streets being paved with gold. In America all we desired was an opportunity for a decent family life, a chance to work and an opportunity to accomplish something for ourselves.

We were still at a very tender young age, we had barely survived the camps in a horrible physical and mental condition trying to recoup our health but somewhat still weak and not knowing from one moment to another whether or if ever we would ever gain back our normal lives or health. By now we were sure we could not get back our parents who perished in the extermination camps because of that we just wanted to be reunited with out precious Uncles and Aunts, remnants of our families, the brothers or sisters of our beloved parents, so we could get our lives back on the right track and move forward with my life. After all, I was already 21 years old, yet without being settled in a home or country.

The first few days after takeoff the ocean was very rough but a few days on the ocean, it was getting smoother especially as we were getting closer to the American shores it felt great, I had a wonderful time, a loving upbeat feeling of being free and on the beautiful boat, getting where I dreamed all my life I wanted to be.

I could hardly wait for the opportunity to meet our wonderful relatives especially our American Aunts, Uncles, cousins and of course to see our brothers and sister and hopefully have an opportunity or chance soon for a good job, maybe in the profession that I was trained for as a contact lens specialist while I was in England. I had been taught by example from the time I was a child, from our parents and grandparents, that honest hard work brought its rewards, and I was looking forward to working and living in freedom, practicing my religion, or what I remember of it, hopefully to become the best person that I could be and even thought I should try to help others if and when ever possible.

After five days of great fun on the choppy sea, which made most people very sick, we were finally getting close to our destination, which were the shores of New York City, America. I was one of the lucky ones not to become seasick while the huge ship slipped through the often rough stormy December seas. The excitement of soon reaching shores, landing and touching the American soil and finally seeing and meeting my American relatives, getting to know America, it's people was overwhelming, and above all, I was going to be the best man in brother Ben's and his bride Sylvia's wedding in Pittsburgh, PA the day after my arrival. I had no idea how far Pittsburgh was from New York City.

Making new friends on the ship had reached a peak, it was wonderful for me, and now I could think of nothing but reaching my dreamed of destination, anxiously looking forward to seeing meeting, hugging and kissing Aunt Rose, Mothers sister in New York and others in my new American family and of course getting together with my brothers whom I have not seen for several years and my only sister Rosalyn, who came about a year before me, also my sister-in-law, Ruthie, and my new nephew, Eddy. I could hardly wait to meet them in America.

Our arrival in the New York harbor was like a long over due dream come true. Coming to America had been my dream and in my hopes and prayers for so long, since I was eight years old, and after going through so much hunger, torture, abuse and to many, near death situations and sicknesses in the extermination camps. Not so long ago it was hardly believable. No wonder I was so excited when we were close and getting ready to arrive at the port for disembarkation.

I could not believe that it was finally happening, that it was really true. It was still dark, but the Statue of Liberty radiated in all her glory to us. To me the New York lights sparkled like diamonds, gold and rubies combined Of course the Statue of Liberty was a pinnacle of splendor so great that she was breathtaking, and now I could hardly wait for daylight so I could get off the ship to touch and kiss the ground of America "The beautiful bastion of freedom and opportunity," especially for me and my family. I realized and appreciated that America was haven for everyone no matter what race, religion, nationality and that included this condemned Jewish boy, who not so long ago somehow endured and survived the worst hell and sufferings on this earth.

My arriving in New York was marred only because I could not help but focus my thoughts about my perished wonderful parents and others that were murdered so terribly and inhumanely in Auschwitz and what my arrival in America would have meant to them. They would have been overjoyed to know that the "Lady Liberty" was to be the guardian of their children. Never would my parents have suspected that all of their children would miraculously survive and eventually be able to immigrate to call this new land their home. I was delighted not just of the present generation, but for our future generations as well. Now my long precious dream and wish was really beginning to become a reality, and I wished only that our dear beloved parents could have survived the Holocaust to be here so they could enjoy it with us. Hitler and his fascists' cohorts had robbed them and us of their and our dreams when he took their lives in Auschwitz, and he robbed us from being able to show our parents our gratitude how much we really appreciated them for what they did for us, God rest their souls.

Our parents often talked to us about our wonderful relatives, their brothers and sister, our uncles and aunts that are in the golden land of America. Father had two brothers who had wives and children, one of our Uncles his brother passed away and our mother had four brothers and one sister alive with many cousins in America. They all came to America when they were quite young, in the early 1920's all my other Aunts and Uncles on Fathers and Mothers side that stayed in Europe perished in Auschwitz along with most of their children, our cousins.

Most of us were not born yet when they left for America. We looked upon our American relatives as our guardian angles. We hoped that they would be able to help guide us to a complete recovery health wise and help us get on the road to a tranquil normal decent American life. These were my fondest hopes and wished as I got ready to disembark in Ellis Island on American soil from the stately huge ship.

Moments after leaving the Queen Mary, as I walked down the plank, I immediately went down on my hands and knees I cried, prayed and kissed the American soil, soon thereafter I thought I heard a porter paging me. My mother's sister, our precious Aunt Rose Meyers, (may she rest in peace) sent someone to look for me. They were having difficulty in finding me because they were looking for a tall young man at least 5ft. 10inches tall, of normal weight, having thick blond hair and a mustache. The porters were calling for "Mr. Goos," he was looking for me but was mispronouncing my name or saying it a different way, Gross in a New York, Yankee slang. I asked if it was Gross but he ignored me. Then others came to look for me again mispronouncing my name.

I had to talk to several porters before I could convince one of them that I might be the person they were looking for. I realized that they were having difficulty believing me because I certainly did not fit the description that my precious Aunt Rose had given the porter-messenger. I had shrunk a few inches in the camps, and even though I had gained back most of the weight and some of my height that I lost while I was in the camps, (I only weighed somewhere around 60 pounds when I was liberated in Buchenwald),now I weighed around 110 pounds when I landed, also I was only 5'8" not 5'10" or taller and I no longer had a mustache. Finally I was able to convince one of the porters to take me to the gate to meet them There I met for the first time my wonderful Aunt Rose, who resembled in so many ways her sister, our precious, beloved mother. She was with our Uncle Aaron Gross, my father's brother who brought her here to pick me up from the ship.

When I saw them I was overcome with tears of happiness, they started crying also when they saw me. Aunt Rose could not believe that I was not taller or older. She said "Oy-Vey, I thought you were much taller." I was stunned many times by her angelic behavior, her smile and resemblance of our beloved mother, was heart warningly wonderful. Aunt Rose was always good to me, to my brothers and sister and we cherished her, loved her and tried to be good to her, up until she died and left this earth. First I was flying to New York when she lived there many times, then to Miami after she retired and moved there, finally visiting her often in her old age, until the day she died and joined my beloved Mother and other loved ones, no doubt in Heaven. Aunt rose, when I arrived, was still living in Brooklyn, New York and Uncle Aaron lived in Long Island, New York. I was touched and felt very important that they had both come to the docks to welcome and pick me up. It took a while for me to be cleared through the immigration department. I bid my friends who came on the ship with me from the orphanage and Primrose Club farewell, as well as my new friend that I made on the ship, then I gathered my one and only suitcase and left arm-in-arm with my newly found family, we went to Uncle Aaron's automobile in the parking lot; just seeing so many cars and activity in New York, I thought was heavenly beautiful.

As Uncle Aaron drove us away from the busy harbor I was amazed at the many hundreds of automobiles I saw that day in New York. Added to these were so many buses, taxis, trucks, and vans, jammed, people honking; the streets of New York were bustling as usual. I thought what an exciting, bustling city. New York, America, where my new home, new future life was to be. What a wonderful country, yet it is full of excitement. It made me feel great. There was so much traffic that I could hardly believe my eyes, I never thought that there were so many vehicles in the entire world let alone in one city. What I saw of New York upon my arrival was very uplifting to me. We had so few automobiles in Europe and of course none especially in the backward area where I came from or in the adjoining villages or town in the Carpathian, Russia area.

Where I was born and raised as a young boy most of the residents walked to and from work or whatever you had to do and a few had a horse or cattle to pull the wagons they rode on. Some fortunate ones rode bicycles, while most others walked for miles to and from their destinations to and from villages and towns. The vast majority of automobiles that were seen in our area were military vehicles going to and from the man made mountains bastion next to our village or the large military base which was located on the way to the adjoining city of Munkach or later we saw German military vehicles on the way to the Polish, Russian borders or fighting front.

I was especially in awe of the many tall buildings in New York. They seemed much taller and bigger than I ever expected. It looked even taller than the highest mountains close to our village that I had seen in my life before. I was overwhelmed to be in such a bustling place. It seemed that New Yorker's had very little patience, everyone was in such a great hurry to get to where they were going, blowing horns, screaming, and cutting in front of each other. Patience was not displayed by New Yorkers in New York City but it was great to finally be here in America.

As he drove us along the busy New York streets, my Uncle Aaron pointed to one of the buildings. Then he pointed to a few others, saying "that's mine." I felt that he was giving me the impression that he owned these buildings, but it turned out he only had the contract to clean the windows and the interiors of the offices in those buildings. He owned a contracting business that cleaned windows and offices in some of the tallest skyscrapers in New York. I was very proud of him, just as proud as if he actually owned the buildings. His self-confidence was evident and I listened with great interest as he recounted his achievements. He kept saying to me "Just look at what you can accomplish in America when you work hard and put your mind to it." I was hoping for a chance so I could put my mind and energy to accomplish something with my life.

I was truly thrilled to be in the "Big Apple", New York City. Not only because finally my fondest dream was achieved to be with my family in America, but now I felt I was also in the most exciting country in the world. After an overnight stay with our Aunt Rose in New York, Uncle Aaron and Aunt Rose and I left first thing, very early next morning driving to Pittsburgh, PA where my brothers Ben and Bill lived. Bernie, his wife and son, Eddy our first nephew lived close by in Ellwood City PA, and our only sister Rosalyn was by then married, she and her husband were living about 100 miles from Pittsburgh in Erie, PA, I could hardly wait to see all of our disjointed family and especially meet the rest of my American Uncles, Aunts, cousins and other relatives. After all they were the only Uncles and Aunts alive that were not killed in Auschwitz.

It had been a long time since we had been together with our brothers we have not seen or talks to each other for years. Not only was I going to Pittsburgh to rejoin my family that I had not seen for such a long time. Even more important for the first time to be united with my American Uncles, Aunts, and their children, my cousins, whom I had never met.

I was proud to have been asked to be the best man in my brother Ben's and Sylvia's wedding. He arrived in the United States almost a year before me, where he met and fell in love with a lovely, wonderful girl by the name of Sylvia Smooke, whose parents or grandparents were originally from our area of the old country. I felt much honored that they asked me to be the Best Man in their wedding. I will always have special feelings and love Sylvia, and her family, because they waited until I reached America before they got married, so I could have this special honor in their blessed marriage, she and her family were wonderful people and always will be very special to me even though they passed away many years ago.

The ride to Pittsburgh from New York was seven to eight hours by car with one or two stops for bathroom, food and gas. I spent the entire time talking to and hugging my precious Aunt Rose and probing Uncle Aaron, asking them all kinds of questions with my limited English or Yiddish about life in the United States. They answered questions forthrightly and more. They told me about the good and bad things that were happening on this side of the Atlantic, but they emphasized the good positive things, especially the opportunities to get a job and make a good living in a good equal opportunity place in a safe heaven country. Then, too, there was the special times to look forward to, like being together for the holidays, being with family, sharing their joys and being there for them in times of need, as well as help each other realizing the future opportunities.

Time passed very fast on this trip. I will never forget the excitement of arriving in Pittsburgh. I could not help but notice the tall smoke stacks of the steel mills. In December 17, 1949, they were still belching out dark smoke and everything seemed a little sooty. I had an uneasy, scary, awful feeling at first when I saw the black smoke coming out of the tall chimney stacks but I soon realized there was no putrid smell from these stacks like we had been exposed to from the ovens burning humans which was the smell coming from the chimneys at Auschwitz. This smoke was from coal, used for making steel, not from burning the bodies of our families who were killed, then burning our families' human flesh reducing them to smoke and ashes.

Somehow I got my composure back especially because the rolling landscape with nice homes on the side of the Mountains. I soon relaxed and looked forward to meeting my extended family, our beloved parents brothers, that my parents many times had told us so much about; especially our wonderful uncles, aunts their children, as well as my new sister in law, Sylvia's family.

Sylvia's parents, the Smooke family, lived in Pittsburgh, but the wedding took place in nearby Homestead, PA, a suburb of Pittsburgh. The synagogue was very traditional, old and beautiful. I understood the Smooke family had attended this synagogue for many years. The wedding was truly a beautiful exciting occasion for me meeting and getting to know my new found American family, Our only regret was that our beloved dear parents and so many of our dearly-beloved aunts, uncles, cousins and other family members that stayed in Europe and perished during the Holocaust, I wish they could have also lived to be here with us to see and experience this wonderful day of music, singing, dancing, marriage and Yiddish songs, we danced the Horas, which they would have loved.

Of course, especially missed were our beloved Mother and Father, who went up in smoke in Auschwitz, "God rest their souls." Also missed were our brother Philip, his wife and family. They were still trapped in the old village adjoining the town we came from; which had become part of Communist Russia, and the area was renamed Zakarpatska, Ukraine. Philip and his family would not get permission to leave from the Soviet Union for another 25 years. We felt that our parents must be looking down from heaven with pride and joy in this happy union.

Sylvia and Ben was a lovely bride and groom and were truly a happy couple. Sylvia was a wonderful addition to our family and instantly became one of us, as I am sure we became part of her. She was and is a warm and loving person, very devoted to Ben and the family since then. She and Ben have brought up four wonderful children and they each have a special place in my heart. When their first child, our niece, Cindy, was born, I was already in the Korean War, drafted in the US Army stationed in Ft. Meade, MD. I came as soon as boot camp was over and I was able to get some weekend leave. I had no money, but a G.I. who was in basic training with us gave me a ride for the weekend to Pittsburgh just for sharing the gasoline expense. If I had to walk to their home in Pittsburgh I would have done so, just to share in their new joy at the birth of their first child, Cindy was one of the loveliest baby girls I ever held in my hands till then. Since then I have been blessed with many more wonderful nephews and nieces.

The Smooke family, her mother, father and grandparents would eventually pass away (may they rest in peace). Our families have always been very close and we continue to remain close even today. We have always shared in their joys and their sorrows. I arrived in Pittsburgh the evening before the wedding.

Finally excitedly I met and got to know, and fell in love with my dear aunts, uncles and a few of the many cousins in America that I met for the first time that night. I felt truly blessed. I was so glad to be related to these wonderful people. After the good time at the absolutely wonderful wedding, we left that night for Ellwood City, PA, where most of my aunts, uncles, cousins, Brother Bernie and Ruthie lived with their three year old son Eddy. Each of them made me feel welcome in their homes. They gave me the guidance from their heart that I needed and they encouraged me to be a good Jew, a good human, and a loyal America. Because of this guidance I felt that I could never be a disappointment to them or to myself. I felt I had to succeed and have continuously tried since then to be a good person, good American and try to do my best for others.

After getting to meet and know my wonderful family, I personally felt so overjoyed that I could handle anything that life had to offer me in this new land. I know that my beloved parents looked down upon me from heaven above they loved and appreciated there America, brothers, their sister, and their families even more for embracing us in America in the warm, loving manner that they did. We were finally feeling genuinely loved and secure again after having to endure so much horror in the camps, surviving such a dark period of horrific suffering as we did during the Holocaust. Unfortunately, we endured such tragedies and hardships at such a young age that it cannot fully be described and should never be experienced by anyone. Fortunately with the Almighty's help we are in the blessed country of America ready to begin a new life and hopefully make the best of it through honest hard work, and determination to try to accomplish something with my life. I was really looking forward to begin my life in this new country, new world with optimism for the opportunities that lay ahead.

Ellwood City was a very small town next to New Castle, Beaver Falls as well as Pittsburgh, PA close to the Ohio border and Youngstown-Warren, Ohio where most of our business was to expand and grow to be a well known public company.

Chapter 7: Best Memories

I was happy to be inducted into the United States Army soon after I got back to Ellwood City, PA, from Chicago, IL. On February 29, 1951 I, and several other draftees, left New Castle, PA immediately on a train for Ft. Mead, MD, where I would be processed and receive my basic training. As soon as we arrived there I ran across other fellow survivors who were also inducted. After learning from a refugee I knew from the orphanage home in England, that language testing would be given for the Army Intelligence Units, I was asked quickly, so I went up to take the test. These tests were very hard and I was proud when I looked at the scores. My name was near the top of the lost of those that took the test. The trill of passing was truly like a great achievement for me in my desire to serve America.

Meanwhile there was a Czech doctor, a Captain who was very nice to me after I was examined physically, he had me help out where the recruits were arriving in bunches to receive their medical check ups. They would take blood samples by pricking the finger and storing or placing it on a piece of glass. After that the new recruits were sent to my post for what we called "short arm," or genital inspection. I saw an entire college football and basketball team being drafted and being processed. I found out later there had been some irregularity in recruiting and cheating by the students, which caused the entire team to be suspended form school, so they were all drafted and inducted in the Army. As they stood in line watching the blood being drawn, suddenly they started passing out. It was quite funny to watch all these big tough muscular guys, all over six feet in height, falling like dominoes. You could not help but grin at that unbelievable scene.

Not long after this incident, I was assigned to the Army Intelligence Unit, even before my basic training began. Naturally the first six weeks of basic training was very hectic, designed to get young men into shape both physically and mentally. There are so many things to learn but the most important factor is to teach young people discipline, how to take and carry out orders. While in training of course we learned how to march, salute, become orderly, handle discipline, learn to shoot, take apart and clean all kinds of weapons, such as machine guns, rifles, pistols even heavy weapons. Training also included getting in shape and how to survive long marches in all kinds of weather, and how to find your way in an obstacle course. None of these things were as important as carrying our orders smartly and quickly when given by a superior, they also made us realize that it is important, not only during combat, but during all times to follow instructions very carefully and promptly, especially in the Army Intelligence Unit.

I was pleased and proud to be in the Intelligence Unit. I believed that I was fortunate to serve with the best military people in the world. Our unit consisted mostly of reserve officers and non-commissioned officers. At that time most soldiers felt honored to serve their country, but with me it was two-fold. It was a blessing beyond my greatest dream. I heard of the "Terrible Drill Instructors," but I must say that our instructors were not at all as tough as I had heard. Maybe I accepted their gentle screaming and verbal abuse better than most, because it was not the horrible inhuman treatment that received whilst I was in the Nazi Concentrations camps during World War II. Our Drill Instructors seemed like angels compared to the SS Officers, Capos, Blockelsters and guards in the concentration camps I was in during World War II which was only a few years ago.

The Drill Instructors were basically good men whose job it was to get us young recruits into shape and to make us into potentially good soldiers and fighting men. Most of the young men had come directly without experience from their parents homes into the military. No doubt a lot of them had lived sheltered lives and had seldom been screamed at. Here the Drill instructors job was to make them tough and ready to accept orders at a moments notice and be ready for combat, because their very lives would depend on it.

There was no room for questions or errors in a soldier's life. All of us simply had to become tough, to have a military sixth sense about our self in order to survive and do our duty. This was the job of the basic training Drill Instructors. When others put the Drill Instructors down or questioned their every order as abuse, I tried to explain to them that they were not being overly tough or strict but were simply trying to get us ready for military service. Many of the recruits could never understand it when I told then how "good" our treatment was compared to what we experienced at the hands of the Nazis.

Even though I enjoyed Basic Training I still suffered from the memories of the abuse that we took at the hands of the Nazis.

Sometimes when and extremely loud command was heard I would shiver, as the painful memories arose. My mind could not hide, even though I tried to forget the extreme punishment I received. What I had to live through in the concentration camps I tried to blank out these memories or to push them so far back into my memory bank that didn't want to have to deal with them. I wanted to be like all of the other recruits that were born in America. I wanted to have a clear mind and body to serve proudly the United States of America, the country I loved to the best of my ability.

While serving in the Intelligence Units immediately after basic training, I was given the opportunity and asked to serve and be shipped to Europe. I requested, instead of Europe, to remain in the United States or go to the Korean front lines to fight. Partly because I could not yet face stepping on the bloodied Eastern European soil especially Germany at the time. The horrors that I experienced from those fascists were still too fresh in my mind. I could close my eyes and hear the screaming, my nostrils would fill with the acrid smell of dead bodies of people dying and stacked up all around me, the putrid smell of the gas chambers and the crematoriums. I knew it would take many, many years before I could think of or want to return to Eastern Europe. I also did not know what to expect or how I would react, if I did return to Europe and ran into one of the former SS officers or guards from the concentration camp. What would my reaction be? Could I contain myself or would I loose my cool and over react? I was grateful that I was reassigned to a new outfit and did not have to go back to Europe; as a result they assigned me to another base.

Our sergeant's name was Royster and he was rumored to be as "tough as nails." Well, he might have appeared to be strict to others. I seemed to get along just fine with him, better than most of the other recruits because I was totally obedient and "on the ball." He picked me to be his personal jeep driver, even though I had never passed a drivers test and had no driver's license.

I enjoyed the extra duty of taking care of him for many reasons. I often drove him into the city of Baltimore for an evening of pleasure. Once when we were in a Baltimore strip club, I noticed a strip dancer who has a gorgeous face and body. She seemed to be having trouble with her contact lenses, she kept blinking and rubbing her eyes but she had a sweet face. Not too many people knew how to fit or make contact lenses in those days. Sergeant Royster also noticed the dancer, but obviously for other reasons. She was a very good looking young woman with a very sexy body. I called her over then introduced myself to her as she got off stage and told her that I was a contact lens specialist, that I would be honored if she would allow me to adjust them to fit her eyes better, most of all I wanted my sergeant to meet her and spend some time with her. She agreed, we all got along fine as a result. We made several trips into Baltimore, supposedly to adjust her lenses, but most of all for the sergeant's relaxation. They had a good time when I was trying to find a place to fix her contact lenses.

I told her about my extensive experience making contact lenses in England and Chicago, as well as adjustments of contact lenses in London to make them fit her eyes better. I volunteered to go with her to her optometrist to adjust the lenses for her. As a result, she, the sergeant and I became good companions. I was able to help her and also started to work out an arrangement with the eye doctor for a part-time job for myself. Needless to say, I got a few free pleasure breaks for the sergeant.

I enjoyed basic training, even more after that especially the trips to Baltimore. I was fortunate to make some good friends. I also met several more boys who were with me in England, that were also survivors from the camps. We were able to remember and talk about our good times in the orphanages in England and Scotland. We talked about our buddies that we had not seen since we left England or arriving in America. Most of us were assigned to the Military Police for training with boys, most of them were from Kentucky, who were tall and excellent marksman.

At the end of basic training, I was selected and assigned to the M.I.S. 210 Censorship section of the Intelligence, because of my ability to communicate in six languages, my knowledge of people in Eastern Europe where communism was trying to emerge like Hitlerism to conquer the people of Europe and indeed the world and especially because of my experience with those countries and terrain. I felt much honored to be selected for the Intelligence Unit and maybe there would also be a potential opportunity to work in the optical fiend, hopefully with contact lenses for the Medical Corp.

I took advantage every time I could of getting to know people; men and women who served with me in the US Armed Forces as well as the civilian around our bases. In basic training I felt fortunate that we had boys from every part of America in our units. Some of the boys were city-bred, others country-bred. It was amazing to see the differences in them. The northerners were so different in some ways from the Southerners. Their uniqueness was sometimes humorous to see. I did not realize just how much difference there was in people from the cities or the country, or people from the north, ease, south or west, no matter where or who they came from, it was beautiful to see how they blend in our or how many things they have in common in spite of difference customs, habits, drawls, dialect, etc. Some of the soldiers probably had never been outside their village, city or county, some had never seen the ocean and others had never seen the prairie states. To me it was great to know that in America, there were people rich, poor, and from all walks of life, color and religions under one roof and getting along.

We pow-wowed and tried to get to know each other checked each other out before fully understanding each other. Their cultures were so different, even their dialects were different from one another. This made me feel less of an outsider, as my broken, limited English was still very bad, certainly not good enough to be understood by most, or the way I should have been understood in order to get on in America. I began to understand more than I could speak. We often laughed at each other, when I would try to explain something. We used sigh language sometimes to make ourselves understood. The camaraderie was great; we learned to look after each other. Soon our basic training was over and because I did not desire to go back to Europe, I was assigned back with the 210 Censorship Unit. Soon our entire outfit was transferred, and then ordered to leave within a few days for Ft. Bragg, N.C. for other assignments.

Just at that time my brother Ben and his wife Sylvia blessed us with a new baby girl, their first child, so I hustled and pulled some strings to get a long week-end pass and fortunately was able to arrange with a fellow GI for a ride to Pittsburgh, PA. And back by sharing in the cost of gasoline as I had no car. I was in Seventh heaven when we got there, I immediately picked the baby up and loved holding and kissing my precious baby niece, Cindy and being with the family. I also enjoyed a few good home cooked scrumptious meals, rather than basic training food, unfortunately I had to get back to Mead quickly because the day after I got back we were on our way with the convoy driving sough from Ft. Meade, MD, to Ft. Bragg. We went through some real nice cities and beautiful country side. We saw some beautiful rivers and hilly train. When we got further south, pretty close to Atlanta, I was very impressed with the weather, the Southern hospitality and the area in general. Finally, we arrived in Ft. Bragg, NC. I fell in love with the South.

It was at the height of the Korean War. Training was getting intensified. They were trying to teach us all kinds of Intelligence, as well as, military methods in Ft. Bragg: even parachuting. I was taken up a very tall tower and ordered to glide down, which was supposed to feel like a parachute fall or drop. I did not like it, but was told to do so. Now we were attached to the 82nd Paratroop Airborne Division for training, but we were still in the U.S. Army Intelligence.

Right after that, because our section was not part of 112 Intelligence censorship and Interrogation Unit, and we were assigned to partake in the biggest maneuvers ever, which was called Maneuvers Southern Pine in preparation for the most massive airborne assault training for the largest offensive airborne drop soon in Korea. Several airborne divisions, as well as the Air Force, Army, Marines, Navy and others took part in these maneuvers.

Some of us in our section were going over some intelligence procedures, as well as reviewing the censorship procedures we needed to put into place for enforcement in a big tent we set up headquarters which we had pitched in the forest. While others were laying out their individual sleeping tent, in wetlands, on the mushy forest ground, we were busy with our serious discussions, what we can do and what we should do, when suddenly one of our men, a tall handsome corporal, who was a Christian, of Arab origin, from Palestine, came rushing in trying to tell us something. He was a good friend and a fine young attorney from Boston. I immediately shook him and tried to make him rational. He started to point to the outside and tried to say something and mumbled the word "shh tent…moving." I asked him to slow down and tell me what was wrong. He pointed to the area where he had tried to put his tent on the ground. On one end of the tent the floor of the tent was moving. We yanked the tent and out came a rattle snake, still moving and hissing, his head in the air and spraying venom at everyone. His tail was still rattling. The snake must have been 10 to 12 feet long. Most people were scared to go near it; I was looking for a regular rifle or gun with bullets. All we had as part of the Intelligence Group was a hand gun. With no bullets.

I ran over to the Military Police, close by, to borrow an M-I or M-2 rifle with Dum-dum bullets. One of the M.P. came with us. He was a good ole boy from Kentucky who had taken basic training with us. He started pumping bullets into the snakes head. Even after emptying several rounds, the tail was still moving. Of course, this gave most of us great concern, because we were sleeping this forest on bare ground with just a blanket on the ground and one to cover us from the evening chill and a tent over our heads. We were scared for a good reason for after raking the pine straw and leaves from our sleeping area, which was a sort of wetland, we realized that other snakes could come after us during our sleep. We did not realize that they only attack if they are disturbed. Once we were informed of this we did not want to disturb them of course if they had asked us we would tell them so. Needless to say we not get much sleep that night.

The incident with the snake made us cautious with everything we saw in the forest. Even in our work we managed to discover through careful interrogation of so-called prisoners, and our censorship, people checking carefully the wind, weather, and other intelligence work that we discovered that the so called enemy lines were very close to and behind us. We had to concern ourselves with imaginary spies, counter intelligence, opposition, and censorship; as well as wind and weather predictions.

When we got the latest weather report about a strong wind that was supposed to arrive at the same time as the so-called enemy drop was to occur very early in the morning which could lead the so called enemy troops away from the clear landing zone into a wooded, snake infested, swampy area after all they were our own U.S. Airborne boys even though they were supposed to be the enemy, from another outfit and base. We did not really want them to be hurt. We brought it immediately to the attention of our superior officers. We pleaded with them to postpone move the drop area a few hundred feet. We even urged them to cancel the air maneuvers for awhile because of the anticipated wind, but we were totally ignored. When the designated time arrived they called the jump and the paratroopers were pushed into the dangerously wooded swampy snake infested area, it was not a pretty sight to see our American boys stuck handing in tall pine trees with their parachutes caught in the branches, or laying in the swamps with the poisonous snakes around them.

By the time they could be rescued there were quite a few serious casualties. These could have been avoided if the commanding officers had listened and paid attention and check out our information. It was heartbreaking to see so many young men injured, or god forbid killed, especially when we were sure many of them would be hurt unnecessarily. We felt crushed, because unfortunately, they could have been saved. If only we could have held the drop us for a couple of hours, or moved it a couple hundred feet, a tragedy could have been avoided. We assisted as best as we could to get them out of the trees and out of the swamp, but for some of them it was too late, we were not able to move around the swamp very fast and we were scared. But we helped a little.

The food during the maneuvers was fairly good but we still looked forward the Army canteen trucks that came just after lunch. We could buy a coke, tea, crackers, candy or chewing gum, or even cigarettes. We formed lines to buy what our limited money would allow us to buy. I was getting about $80 a month as a Private First Class, and felt that I was able to afford these things on my pay.

Even in those days in the U.S. Army we had anti-Semites. One of the corporals in the new outfit which I was attached to was from Italy, but born in America of Italian descent. His parents moved back to the old country because they were Nazi sympathizers before the war. He was one of Mussolini's fascist. He also claimed to be anti communist and openly did not like the Jews. Because I served in the same outfit with him and I was Jewish, he baited me every opportunity that he had. He was always threatening to finish the job that Hitler started and had not been able to finish, to get rid of the Jews which included me.

On a maneuver one time, just after lunch, the canteen truck arrived as we were standing in line to but a coke and candy. I was right behind this corporal. As he was bragging that he was born in America, but during the war he had lived in Italy, very proud that he was in the Deuce fascist or Hitler Youth Group, and he made all kinds of fascist, anti-Jewish remarks. He even bragged about being happy about how they had tortured and deported Jews of his area of Italy to the German Concentration camps and that he hoped that he would soon see the same fate for the Jews of American as for the Jews of Europe.

I first asked him nicely to stop egging me one with the anti-Semitic remarks and threats. Then I especially warned him to stop harassing and baiting me as we stood in line. There was a large group of men about. No one spoke to him and told him to stop or to try to defend me against this hateful anti-Semitic. He was always looking for a fight or to beat me. He stepped on my foot and bumped into me on purpose a few times. In a nice way I continued to tell him to leave me alone, but this to no avail because he was a corporal and I was just a private.

Suddenly, as he was playing with is money he dropped some of his change on the hot sand. Accidentally, and on purpose, I stepped on his hand and the hot summer sand burned his hand. He started to scream, to kick me and to punch me. He was cursing me and calling me a "bloody S.O.B. Jew." He said as loudly as he could that he would finish what Hitler had failed to do, which was to get rid of the Jews. I warned him in a loud clear voice to make sure that everyone heard me to shut up, but he continues to punch me and to kick me. I went into a boxing pose and with a couple of left defensive jabs and a right hood, he went down. When he got up he attacked me again, so I got in a few more solid punches, which hurt my wrist, and then I utilized my soccer experienced feet and kicked him hard a few times. I managed to punch him a few more times which knocked him our cold. I helped to carry him to the medic tent, besides a sore jaw and a few other sore sports, he was okay. I believed that he learned his lesson not to mess with me or any other Jew. The reputation went around quickly not to mess with this Alex, the Jew boy.

The only other confrontation that I had in the army was with a master sergeant from the same outfit I was assigned to. He was an Arab and fiercely hated Jews. He especially hated me because he found out that I had a brother who went to Israel to fight for Jewish statehood in Palestine. Unfortunately I had not heard from my brother Sam for a long time about how he was doing since suffering a very serious injury at the Egyptian front.

No matter what those couple of incidents might suggest, there is no doubt that I served under some great officers and non-commissioned officers. I enjoyed every minute of my stint in the Army, except for a few incidents from the time that I was transferred into a new outfit in Ft Bragg, from censorship to interrogation. Serving under a Major who was not too friendly to us, and his Arab Master Sergeant, who was against a Jewish state in Palestine, He let me know, without saying a word, that he hated all Jews.

When word reached him that I had a brother in the Israel military he made life more difficult. I had been tormented by masters of the worst kind in the extermination camps, and this was just another incident of hate and bigotry on the part of a person. I was sure that they did not have the backing of the U.S. government or the military, much less the American people in general. Therefore I tried to stay away from him whenever possible. The master sergeant assigned me extra evening work details and extra duty almost every weekend, but I tried to put up with it hoping that it would stop or that he would change.

I remember one weekend in particular, when I had plans to go into Durham, NC, not too far from Ft. Bragg, with some other G.I.'s from our outfit. It was always fun to get away with a group of soldiers from our base; for the most part they were very nice. One of us would rent a cheap hotel room in town and several of us would stay in it to share the expenses. Since none of us had much money, we were compelled to do this, because in 1953, we only received $84.00 a month as a private and only $112.00 as a corporal. I looked forward to the weekends and anticipated the fun that we would have dancing with the beautiful city girls who really appreciated us soldiers. When the sergeant found out about our plans, and I was included that I would be leaving with the boys he was furious. He tried to stop me by giving me extra work duty that weekend. I was lucky to find another soldier (a corporal originally from Lithuania) to fill in for me and take care of my work detail. He was to haul some metal lockers upstairs in our barracks for me after inspection was over that Saturday afternoon and I was to teach him dancing and introduce him to some girls.

I got dressed in my clean tailor fitted uniform, and proceeded to take the bus and leave for the weekend with my friends. The Sergeant realized that I planned to go anyway; he did not want me to 'run out on him' so I had to sneak out. I waited at the bus stop on the base for bus to arrive ant take us to the city so that I could make a run for it before he realized I was gone. Just before the bus arrived he noticed me and tried to stop me. It was very clear that he was very strong and a bigot to everyone who heard him not just me. A group of paratroopers from the 82nd Airborne, as well as guys from our outfit, who were also waiting for the bus, were attracted by the blasphemy and physical abuse that he was lashing out at me. They encouraged me to fight back, and that the sergeant was out of line. I had on a tight Ike jacket, and the Sergeant grabbed me by the middle.

He pulled my chest hair out as he lifted my 130+ pound frame into the air as he continued to shake and curse me. Finally, I was encouraged by others to fight back so I had to utilize my boxing and soccer skills, plus my fighting ability. Since I has no other choice, I kicked him hard between the legs and while her was bent over in pain I used my best soccer kicks and boxing skills to punch and kick him to finish the job that he had started, even if it was temporary. Laughter and applause was heard from the bystanders. Just as the bus finally arrived and soon I rushed onto the bus and was happy to see the door close behind me before he recovered.

The driver, seeing all the commotion, hurriedly took off out of the base and continued towards Durham at a fast rate of speed. When we arrived at the hotel in Durham, I called my former commander, Major Stern, who was my commander at Ft. Mead and he took us to Ft. Bragg. I explained what had happened and what was going on between the sergeant and me. I pleaded that he speak to my present Major and the commanding officer of the Intelligence Unit on my behalf as I had never been in trouble before. He assured me that he would do just that. In fact, he was going to talk to the commanding officer the colonel of the entire intelligence unit that day. He set up a hearing as soon as I got back Monday morning he had the military guard meet me and escort me and I was given an opportunity to explain what happened between the sergeant and myself. At the hearing, witness after witness came forth in my behalf and corroborated my story of how he was picking on me, the discriminating remarks he made and he extra duty he had given me, and other things he made me do. They told of how he baited me, and how he physically abused me. They also told of how he treated me and kicked me while I was at the bus stop. They were very supportive of me and on my behalf. When the hearing ended, the Sergeant was stripped of his rank and transferred out. After the hearing and the Southern Pine maneuvers were over I requested and was fortunate to be transferred to another outfit, the Medical Corps in St. Louis, MO.

My transfer to St. Louis was a blessing in many ways. Not only did I have a lot of fun there, I managed to save some money, got additional schooling, made lots of friends, and learned in a very short time the American way of doing things. This was the best education that I could have received, better than I could have learned it anywhere. Even in college, if I had been able to afford or could to go. I worked in the Medical-Optical section downtown making eye glasses for the military. I made glasses for the top ranking officer in my unit; I received the highest clearance by the Pentagon because I was in the intelligence.

The barracks were about seven miles away from the town where the optical shop was. The bus would bring us in the morning and take us back after work. I would spend the last thirteen months of my army life in St. Louis, MO, very productively and enjoyed my stay more and more every day.

In those days contact lenses were very new in the U.S, as well as in Europe, and I used the knowledge that I acquired in England and in Chicago to help with the new frontiers in optics. While working in the medical unit, I was honored to make eye glasses for several famous dignitaries, among them several generals. Somehow, I felt that I was thanking them for liberating me from the Nazis. I am almost positive we made glasses for General Eisenhower, President Truman, General MacArthur, etc. Since I had such a high clearance I was assigned to make glasses for the important dignitaries.

Soon I was promoted to Corporal and wore my uniform with even more pride. I wore it most of the time, because it helped me save money not to have to buy civilian clothes, but mostly because of the looks that I received from the girls--- especially on the dance floor. Since Corporal pay was still very low, I had to cut corners on my expenses because I was still trying to send money home to Bill so that he could continue the business that we had started, and I wanted to save money for a car when I got out of active duty from the Army. Of course I realized that I would stay in Reserves for another five years which delighted me.

I spent most of my free time in St. Louis at the USO Club and the YWHA (Young Women's Hebrew Association). We could always count on good food there and cute girls. I was able to go free to the dances because I taught dancing in the various Clubs. The dance clubs gave me the opportunity to spend joyful hours with ladies on the dance floor teaching them how to ballroom Latin dance. I always enjoyed music and ballroom dancing, especially the latest dances. Dancing came naturally to me, I picked it up in England as it was the only entertainment I could afford besides soccer sports, and the girls seemed to enjoy dancing with me just as much as I enjoyed dancing with them.

Shortly after I got to St. Louis one of the dance instructors noticed my dancing ability, and I was offered a part time job teaching dancing for pay in one of the ballrooms two nights a week. I was thrilled to have the opportunity to dance with all kinds of good looking sweet girls, and to make some extra money in the process. My dancing kept on improving with my teaching, so I entered exhibitions and danced in a few competitions in St. Louis, Chicago, as well as gave exhibitions on boats afloat on the Missouri River so I had fun and made money.

I let the word our around St. Louis that I made contact lenses before coming to America and that I had also made them when I lived in Chicago. Someone told me of a company that I should contact as they might be looking for part-time help. I never thought that I would have time for a job in the private sector even though I made glasses for the military and government dignitaries eight hours a day five days a week. I became intrigued with the idea of extra work and real money in my field of optics. Fortunately, I got a job working a few hours a week with eye doctors, helping them to fit and adjust contact lenses. At the same time I was also studying for the G.E.D. high school test and somehow I passed. I got my high school equivalent diploma. This enabled me to enter college to take evening classes. For this I was very grateful even though it meant working and studying seven days and evenings each week.

With the extra money form my part time job, and the G.E.D. diploma I enrolled at Washington University in St. Louis, where I took a course in Logic two nights a week. My calendar was full. I worked two nights a week teaching doctors how to fit contact lenses and taught dancing two nights a week, two more nights a week in class in Washington University. This only left me Saturday night for dating, dancing and relaxation. Needless to say I dated very little and spent most of my time only with very nice girls who provided transportation, helped me with my English, were good cooks or all of the above. I befriended a lovely girl who helped me with my school, especially English studies. She was a great cook and so was her grandmother, so I had a good place to stay a night or tow each week, especially when I worked or studies late, then she dragged me off to work. We became best of friends but I was not interested in getting serious, even though she was lovely and had a wonderful family. Marriage was the last thing on my mind, and I informed her so.

I enjoyed my Logic classes, which helped me understand later in life the tough business world and family entanglement. I realized that I needed to save more money so that when I got out of the service I would get a basic automobile that I would need to get my life on track. The extra income, working evenings and weekends gave me this extra needed money. I saved most of the; money I made from the dance lesson classes and the contact lens work. It made me feel great to put money away for a rainy day. My two years of active service was nearing the end and I was happy for that but grateful to have served my country. Now I faced only the five years of army reserve duty that was about to begin.

Before I was released to civilian life a letter came for me. The former employer, The Ritzholtz Company, where my friend Jerry Hornstein still worked in Chicago wanted to talk to me about coming back to work for them. He sent me an airplane ticket, and as soon as I got my discharge at Fort Leonard Wood, MO, I first went back to St. Louis for the weekend to say good bye to fellow dancers, workers and many friends that I had made. I left my friends and my girlfriend and made the trip to Chicago. When I got there, Mr. Ben Ritholtz spent the evening with me, and had a leisure lady for me, which I declined. He offered me immediately a good incentive to take the job as manager of his Pittsburgh division office, which was close to the business that I had started with Bill. I left Chicago and was sorry to leave my friend, Jerry Hornstein; I left the next evening with a happy but heavy heart. I left because I was glad to rejoin my family. Bill and I would be able to work part time together again in our business. In Pittsburgh, I was to train eye doctors, optometrist, in the field of fitting contact lenses as well as sell eye glasses.

I explained to my employer that I would work for him only a short time, but that I would return to the business that I had started with Bill as soon as I trained the people and got the business going. My income with him was based on incentives the increase of business I was able to accomplish. So I managed to achieve a 50% increase almost every week from the previous week, after a couple of months I had the cash I needed for the car (with the money I had saved while in the Military) and the confidence I needed to succeed in our business. I found and trained a good management replacement and other good employees to assure the business would be successful, therefore, I left it in good shape and graces most of all I had saved up $1,760.00 in a savings account.

As soon as I got back to Ellwood City, my uncle took me to a car dealer, where I bought a new stripped down version of a 1953 two door Chevrolet for which I paid $1,720.00 cash which left me with $40.00 to live on. I was proud of my first new car. When I slid behind the wheel at the dealership, I felt like a king. To me it was like a Rolls Royce, very luxurious, even though it did not have a heater, radio or any of the luxury things we have in cars today…it was reliable transportation with four wheels which is what mattered and what was needed for me to get back into the business. So I rejoined Bill in Ellwood City and New Castle and planned to expand to adjoining cities in Ohio as soon as possible.

Appendix

Questions frequent every survivor's story and the entire Holocaust as a historical event, chief among them whether the Jews overstate the events of their personal story, and whether the Jewish community collectively has sought to play on the sentiments of six million victims. There was a perception that Hitler used the outcome of the Wannsee Conference to make it appear that he would sell the Jews to the world if the countries were willing to buy. This was never the case, as the chief purpose was to announce the finale of "The Jewish Question," and let contracts be written that would build the death camps, the machinery, the methods, and reinvigorate the German war machine which was brought to a halt after WWI.

The world was in an economic depression. Collectively, many factories were silent for every country in the world. The third question on Hitler's mind was whether the world would object to his policy and quash him. He wanted to redraw most of Europe, a desire that was in violation of the terms of surrender in WWI. He wanted to crush Jewish feelings so he could take their minds and bodies with least resistance. First, he set the machinery in place to build the camps. The gas chambers were still in development, so in many cases a daily quota was shot. The invention of the gas chambers and crematoriums made it possible to exterminate three train loads of passengers in each camp. By using inmates, they could speed up the process even more.

Hitler offered the Jews passage to any country of their choice if they were willing to turn over 75% of their hard assets. The Jews were not told of the mass redesign of immigration quotas worldwide, however. In the U.S., unemployment was so bad that boat loads of passengers were rejected and sent back to Germany, where they were then sent to the death camps. As an example, the Japanese took many and converted them to slaves. The world was not taking the Jews in, with very few exceptions, such as Palestine and Australia for a time. The economic downturn turned out to be a very effective weapon against the Jews. It doomed hopes of freedom for many.

The machinery was ready for the factory of death. Three shifts operating continuously meant the smoke stacks were full of odors of burning flesh. The Nazis took their identity and devalued them even more by letting them know no one would pay a price for them. It was even advanced further that God had rejected them. Elie Wiesel elicits a different interpretation by offering that the will to survive was to build a mass who would testify against the Nazis

"The world survivors speak of has been so rigidly shaped by necessity, and so completely shared – almost all survivors say "we" rather than "I" – that from one report to the next the degree of consistency is unusually high. The facts lie embedded in a fixed configuration; fixed, we may come to believe, by the nature of existence when life is circumscribed by death."[1]

---

[1] Des Pres, Terrance. (1977). *The Survivor.* (1st ed.). New York, NY: Washington Square Press, Page 28

This was the beginning of a fight back to which consensus was built in the minds of the victims so they might collectively rise up on a different plane.

"Their purpose – strong enough to lift the spirit from truly inhuman depths – was to destroy the camp and allow at least one man or woman to escape and bear the tale."[2]

Silence is the real crime against humanity. Again the whole effort was to take away what they heard, and from that, mindful of the truth, this became a way to stand up and protest their state.

"Most accounts of life in the camps appeared on first hearing to be a disconnected series of stories about the critical moments when the narrator nearly died but then miraculously managed to save himself. The whole of camp life was reduced to these highlights, which were intended to show that although it was almost impossible to survive, man's will to live was such that he came through nevertheless. Listening to these accounts, I was horrified at the thought that there might be nobody who could ever properly bear witness to the past. Whether inside or outside the camps, we had all lost our memories. But it later turned out that there were people who had made it their aim from the beginning not only to save themselves, but to survive as witnesses. These relentless keepers of the truth, merging with all the other prisoners, had bided their time-there were probably more such people in the camps than outside, where it was all too common to succumb to the temptation to make terms with reality and live out one's life in peace. Of course those witnesses who have kept a clear memory of the past are

---

2   Des Pres, Page 33

few in number, but their very survival is the best proof that good, not evil, will prevail in the end."[3]

The meticulous nature of their daily task was contained herein. Again, the purpose was always to build a witness. They assumed some would die in their quest to resist. How do you keep the will to survive when the SS keep telling you that resistance is useless?

"Death is compounded by oblivion, and the foundation of humanness – faith in human continuity – is endangered. The final horror is that no one will be left. A survivor of Dachau told me this: 'The SS guards took pleasure in telling us that we had no chance of coming out alive, a point they emphasized with particular relish by insisting that after the war the rest of the world would not believe what happened; there would be rumors, speculations, but no clear evidence, and people would conclude that evil on such a scale was just not possible.'"[4]

The holocaust was processed differently by each of the inmates. This is in part due to the loose nature of torture that was inflicted upon those who were its soon-to-be victims. Those who worked to process the train-loads who came through saw the holocaust differently. They translated their assignment as a chance to witness the reality that lie behind the gate. Their charge was to ensure that every one survive. By working with their captors they could control or in some cases slow the gas chambers processing. Every calculated stand was to build the ability to testify and to bear witness.

---

[3]   Des Pres, Page 35
[4]   Des Pres, Page 36

Personal Afterword from Dr. Ty Busch

Much has happened to me in the ten years since Alex and I were together. I experienced several delays in finishing a Ph. D. program due to what unfolded in my attempt to reenter the Mormon faith. I feel as though I grasped onto the Jewish side of myself in an attempt to stabilize my life. I needed consistency and order in my life, and Judaism gave me that. I could understand my father and mother better now. My brothers always were distant factors in my life, and that's the way it has been since he died.

I began my Jewish experience in mid-life, taking up the burdens and challenges of the Torah without closing the door on Mormonism, in which I had spent 15 years of my life. I was angry with what had transpired, and wanted to take control of my life again. My wife, Donna, was less taken aback, and said that Judaism brought out a softer side of me. A sentiment that wouldn't truly hit me until 2007, when we were swimming in debt and pain due to a hit and run accident that should have killed me. Donna's legs were frail after the surgery and gave out. She needed surgery and we had no insurance to pay for the necessary home care, as we did when my aneurysm had bulged in my belly. The Lord wanted for my survival.

The burdens of Torah fell upon me. The Church would not willingly help, because they wouldn't accept me. I went south and masqueraded as someone else to reinvigorate my membership. The baptism was real and the feeling was great. I prayed each night for the Lord's guidance. Had we left the area, I could have restarted and been someone else in the Church. I made a mistake in returning to Bishop Hanks, and as shocked when he told me that he was a Klansman. Suddenly all of the false sentiment he uttered to me began to fall into place. I would never see membership, and despite that I wanted to fight, but it was no use.

The good thing was that my Judaism is strong, and the Christian perspective infused in me from a young age from the Methodist and Presbyterian faiths became stronger as well, and the future has become somewhat brighter. Donna and I hope for a good tomorrow. It has been an ordeal for us since 1998, and we hope the auto accidents will help put our lives back together so we can wait until December 2010 to file for bankruptcy.

Alex Gross

Alex Gross was born on September 18, 1928 in Czechoslovakia, and lived through its annexation by Hungary and its takeover by Nazi Germany. He was incarcerated at age 14 in a ghetto, and shipped to the extermination camps of Auschwitz, Birkenau, then Buna and Gleiwitz. After being liberated from Buchenwald by the American Army, along with his brothers Bill and Sam, he returned to Czechoslovakia, and found three more brothers and one sister survived. His parents were victims of Auschwitz extermination. As a result he spent some time in orphanages in England, before coming to America on December 16, 1949, to join his surviving family in the United States.

In 1950 he started a construction business with brother, Bill, in 1950. During the Korean war he voluntarily spent two years in the U.S. Army Intelligence & Medical Corps, after which he attended Washington University. He would then join the business with his brothers, Bill, Sam and Ben, who relocated to Atlanta in 1960. The Gross Brothers continued to build every kind of housing; single and multifamily, planned communities, office complexes, and shopping centers in eighteen states.

Married to his wife, Linda, for over 25 years before she was taken from him. Their only son lost his life in a farming accident around the Gross Lake property at the age of fourteen. He has three daughters and one grand-daughter.

He has been the recipient of many awards from Rotary International, Kiwanis International, Lions Club, and schools. Active in many civic and charitable organizations, he served as a Boardmember of the Atlanta Jewish Federation, General Chairman of Israel Bonds Metro Atlanta, past President of HEMSHECH, an organization of Survivors of the Holocaust, was honored by B'nai B'rith, Veterans Organization, O.R.T., and the governor of Georgia. He was awarded the degree of Doctor of Laws, Honoris Causa at Emory University on May 5, 1995.

He has been written up in USA Today, Good Fortune Magazine, New York Times, Nashville, TN, Ohio, florida, Georgia, and Alabama. He has appeared on many television programs, such as Good Morning America, Cable News Network, and local TV stations. A strong supporter of youth sports, and active in health club, soccer, racquet ball, business, and devoted much of his resources to various charities.

Most of all, he was a proud American.

Tyrone Busch

Ty, as friends and acquaintances call him, was born in 1948 in Longview, Washington to working class parents. He was always interested in social action. He is a graduate of Portland State University with BA in Social Science. In 1986 to 1989 the family went to Las Vegas where he earned an MA in Social History at the University of Nevada Las Vegas. He went to University of Cape Town to complete a Ph. D. in Sociology, while pursuing a full teaching career in the US, Canada and campuses worldwide. Meeting Alex Gross connected him to his past.